THE SERPENT'S SHADOW

THE SERPENT'S SHADOW

DANIEL BRAUM

Cemetery Dance Publications
Baltimore
❧ 2023 ❧

Cemetery Dance Publications
132B Industry Lane, Unit #7
Forest Hill, MD 21050
www.cemeterydance.com

PRAISE FOR THE SERPENT'S SHADOW:

"The setting is the real star here, the sweaty, breathing jungle of Cancun and the Yucatan, but the increasing desperation and dread of the characters pulled me in. From the pulsing clubs to the deep cenotes, Braum holds our hands as we dive together into a maze of suspense."

—David Wellington, Author of Monster Island

"An expertly plotted coming-of-age story where love isn't just blind, but horrific."

—Sarah Langan, Author of Audrey's Door

*"*The Serpent's Shadow *is a chilling apocalyptic brew of myth and murder. Daniel Braum immerses the reader in a Mayan paradise torn by spiritual conflict where all roads and rivers lead to a stunning climax."*

—Douglas Wynne, Author of Black January

The Serpent's Shadow *reminds you of the dangers masked in everyday life, how easy it is to step over that unseen threshold dividing the ordinary world into that of pure darkness. It's time for the shedding of skin and the striking of venomous fangs. The Serpent's Shadow is a tale that slithers under your skin and grips you until the last sentence.*

—Michelle Garza, Coauthor of Mayan Blue

PRAISE FOR DANIEL BRAUM'S SHORT STORIES:

"In these deeply melancholic stories, Braum writes of relationships with all the skill of our best realists, but always punctuates and torques his observations with a suspicion of the strange and the unreal. Underworld Dreams *is an original high-wire act that deftly walks the thin line between genres without ever slipping."*

—Brian Evenson

"These dark, genre-blended stories have the same seeming veracity as dreams (no matter what happens, you believe it). The writing is detailed and patient, the characters, original and compelling, and the stories unfold with a sense of strange wonder that leaves a reader in their spell. When you finish one, it's only then you realize you'd been in the underworld, and it's like waking from a nightmare."

—Jeffrey Ford

"Daniel Braum is a true storyteller. By that I mean he spins tales of wonder that grasp at ideas and themes that human beings have been pondering since our brains become up to the task. These stories will also make you laugh, cringe, and damn near weep. This is such a big-hearted and wide ranging book and Daniel Braum is the real deal, a writer to treasure."

—Victor LaValle

INTRODUCTION

I DELIGHT IN stories that deliver more than meets the eye at first glance. I love to read them and I love to write them. *The Serpent's Shadow* is one of those stories.

It is Christmas week. In Mexico, 1987. At first glance all might appear as a "slow-burn" horror tale with familiar tropes. There are teens in peril. Ugly Americans where they should not be. A killer on the loose.

Wander a little further along the road and you might find these tropes you spied at first glance take on new iterations, or may even be subverted. In the jungle you will encounter uncanny visions and strange happenings, a woman who may, or may not, be the incarnation of Santa Muerte / "Saint Death", and even a kaiju big enough to knock the moon out of orbit with the swish of its tail.

My short stories, such as those found in my Cemetery Dance collection *The Night Marchers and Other Strange Tales* operate in the borderlands of the horror genre. While the same can be said for The Serpent's Shadow the quiet horror is punctuated by what might be some of my most brutal and bloodiest depictions. As author Michelle Garza said:

"*The Serpent's Shadow* reminds you of the dangers masked in everyday life, how easy it is to step over that unseen threshold dividing the ordinary world into that of pure darkness. It's time for the shedding of skin and the striking of venomous fangs."

Come now and together we shall enter the jungle. Before we begin there's just one more thing…will you beware the White Lady or will you heed her call?

–Daniel Braum, May 2023.

CHRISTMAS. 1986. CANCUN MEXICO

1.

"HEY, ANSWER ME, space cadet," Regina said. "Wake up!"

My sister's voice eclipsed whatever it was I had been thinking of. Something about space. And the stars. An image of opal green scales faded from my memory. Regina was right. I was staring out our balcony doors at the Mayan ruin on the shore and I...I must have nodded off. I shifted my head and all I saw was glare and the reflection of our fancy hotel room in the glass.

"You know it's true," Regina said. "It's the will of the people that holds civilization together."

My thoughts returned to our verbal sparring. Tonight's round included international economic policies, social philosophy, the World Bank, and the gold standard all mixed together; brought on by our first family trip abroad. Despite the long day of travel I felt all charged up.

"Well, some beliefs are stronger than others," I said. "That's the nature of things. Reality is a shared agreement."

Regina made that exasperated look she reserved for Mom and Dad's more embarrassing parental displays such as blatantly hoarding extra bags of peanuts on the plane ride down here.

She listened at the door to the adjoining room. I could hear Dad's snoring mixed with the roar of the ocean and rustling palms from outside the sliding glass doors that took up most of the living area's wall.

Colorful paintings, stylized beach scenes and wild depictions of the jungle adorned the other walls of the suite. The floors were of polished wood, the paint subdued sand tones. A sleek television and stack of black electronics sat off to the side of the sitting area, the side not facing the view. Everything looked pretty cool, for a resort, not what I was expecting when I heard we'd be staying in a hotel built in the shape of a Mayan pyramid. Easily this was the nicest place I'd ever been. Dad had bartered with one of his rich customers for a week here. He was so excited, our first family vacation since Disneyland when Regina and I were kids. Regina was just excited that everything was going to be so deluxe. Mom was a little too impressed by the note bearing our names wishing us a *Feliz Navidad* by the bowl of foil-wrapped chocolates and candy canes.

I started in again about how everything in society was a battle of intent.

"Shut up, you're going to wake them," Regina said. "One semester of college down and you think you know it all, Mister Philosophy."

"Please tell me you have at least one intelligent cell in your body," I said. "We have a week together."

"If it wasn't for me and my brain cells you'd be going to bed, or just sitting here all night."

She was right, but there was no way I was going to agree with her.

She listened a few seconds longer at the door then said, "Let's go."

A chill ran up my back. Since Dad had announced the trip my head had been filled with stuff from my Meso-American studies class. Mexico's living history and pyramids were all waiting just outside the resort strip. I was finally going to get to touch and taste and feel it all.

THE SERPENT'S SHADOW

We slipped out the door, careful we had the plastic slide key to get back in. The door opened into a courtyard, consisting of a giant pool flanked by two regular looking square hotels and ours between them. Humidity enveloped me; the night air heavy with the salt scent of the sea and flowers. Christmas lights snaked up the clusters of palm trees, illuminating the water and stacked lounge chairs with flashing colors. Two men were cleaning the pool, their faces emotionless as they glanced at us. Both had that sloped Mayan nose and dark, dark hair and eyes.

We dashed to the path leading to the grass lawn behind our building.

"Don't stop till we get to the taxi stand," Regina said, her hands on my shoulders steering me.

"We're guests, no one's going to say anything, right?" I asked.

We both stopped before she could answer. The moon had just risen above the dunes separating the lawn from the beach. I was so glad we were out here where we could hear the ocean, roaring and strong. A line of sand dunes, silhouetted by the moon, ran along the coast as far as I could see. Perched atop a rocky hill in the dunes sat the ruin of a square building, more like a collection of blocks the size of a house, its roofless walls all different heights. Unlike the hulking concrete and stucco mega-structure at our back it looked one hundred percent authentic.

"Wow," Regina said and I was glad she did. We stood there for a few seconds, just taking in its shape against the sea. I knew the Mayan empire was big but I hadn't realized it had stretched all the way to this coast. I wondered if the ruin was real.

"Come on," Regina said and she prodded me onward.

Though it was past eleven the front entrance was still busy. A steady flow of cabs, most little green four-seaters, turned off the strip and rolled up the driveway dropping off sunburned families engorged with dinner and others fresh from the airport still laden in winter clothes. A couple dressed for a night on the town waited on the pick-up line ahead of us. Two Mayan teens about my age staffed the post. Though they wore crisp pink and orange hotel uniforms it wasn't their looks that made them different. They seemed deathly serious. Quieter and more focused than any teen parking cars back home I'd ever seen. That sense of teenage rebellion I was so used to was lacking with them. And it felt very weird. Regina didn't seem to notice.

"Hey," she said to the one not helping the couple into their cab. "We want to go out. What's the best place?"

"The Krystal, ma'am," he said.

I don't think anyone had ever called her ma'am before and she looked bewildered.

"The Krystal is the white hotel," he said, flatly. "The nightclub is the white building outside. Very fancy."

"Let's go," Regina said.

"Kriss-tal" I said, pronouncing the name with a flourish to try and annoy Regina.

"Tell your driver to take you there," he said. "There will be lots of young people, dancing."

The cab with the fancy couple sped away leaving the four of us standing there.

"So," Regina said, drawing the word out. "Are you guys off from school, or what? Where do you go? What are you going to be?"

"To be?" said the kid who called her ma'am.

Regina was always filling empty space with chatter. I had the feeling this *was* their job, this was going to be their life. For a smart ass, and she was smart, a business major with a double minor in economics and math, Regina could be really thick.

"The little temple out by the beach, is it real?" I asked to bail her out.

"Yes," the kid said politely, without a hint of sarcasm or disdain, but I had the impression he had answered this a hundred times before and judged me as some sort of a zero for asking it. I wanted to show him that I knew a thing or two about Mexico and wasn't just some stupid tourist so I switched to Spanish.

"Do you know what it was for?" I asked, in Spanish.

He seemed to think about it genuinely.

"Maybe for the same reasons a hotel is here," he replied, in Spanish. "A nice place by the water?"

The other guy muttered something in Mayan. The speech echoed strangely in my head but I shrugged it off. I knew a few words from class but didn't understand him. He didn't sound friendly. So much for it being a dead language like my teacher said. What else was my teacher wrong about?

Regina switched to Spanish too. Her Spanish was much better than mine and she spoke fast. Sounded like she was a telling a joke and from the few words I caught, a dirty one. When she finished the two just stood there, not even a hint of laughter.

A cab turned off the strip and rolled up the driveway. We got in without further reaction from the two. I yearned to see them crack a smile or something to make me feel normal but the cab just whisked us away.

"Where are you going?" the cabbie asked.

He was a short man with a kind boyish face. His thick moustache made him look older than I thought he likely was.

"The bellhops said the Krystal," I said.

He couldn't hide his disappointment with my answer and looked away to the makeshift altar that had been constructed on his dash; a cross, a plastic Jesus, a stuck-on bud vase with a couple fresh daisies in it, and a figurine of a Mayan woman holding a scythe painted white, the kind I expected to see for sale in every tourist stand.

Was there something wrong with the Krystal? Something he didn't want to tell us?

His face couldn't hide he was struggling with the question. People here were strange. People back home were strange too but easier to size up. Back home you sort of knew where everyone was coming from, because you'd seen them or someone like them before. This cabbie. The pool guys. The bellhops. They were all question marks to me who they really were besides their jobs. They all had uncharted depth. I could feel that depth in this guy. A weight. An anchor tethering him to that depth even though he seemed on the surface carefree.

"La Boom is better," he said. "*Y mas barrato.*"

Cheaper was better Regina and I agreed so La Boom it was.

"Woo-hoo," Regina yelled out the window.

I laughed.

"What?" Regina asked.

"Nothing, just laughing."

"Get ready, tequila's on me, mister," she said. "Merry Christmas, my dear brother."

I noted her sarcasm. Back home Christmas Eve, for us, was for ordering Chinese food from the takeout place and going to see a movie when everyone else was off to big family gatherings. Our family was small. Just us and Mom and Dad and Dad's brother out West somewhere and a few distant relations out there in the world.

"*Feliz Navidad,*" Regina said to the cab driver.

"*Feliz Navidad,*" he said timidly.

"Alright honk your horn and sing along with me," Regina said to him then proceeded to sing.

"*Feliz Navidad…*

Feliz Navidad…

Feliz Navidad y un nuevo ano felicidad."

She jumped right into a chorus of "*bai-ai-la-la la bamba*" which the cab driver found really funny. This was a rare and glorious event—a glimpse of her cutting loose without her zero boyfriend.

THE SERPENT'S SHADOW

This was why I loved her. She could hold her own and mix it up with my philosophical tirades but if it wasn't for her I'd be lost in my own mind and would probably be back in the hotel room like she had said, with the desire but without the gumption to get out and explore the night. I joined in the song and practiced my Spanish by asking questions in Spanish. Simple things. By the time we turned onto the main drag I had learned his name was Tomacito and he was singing right along with us. He was from the Yucatan. The son of a chicle farmer. He had several young children. We cruised onto the strip, the bay on one side, the Gulf of Mexico on the other, a slew of high-rise hotels in-between. Palm trees lit up with Christmas lights were everywhere, lining the road and outside all the night clubs and restaurants flashing that surreal red and green glow on all the modern buildings and the fancily dressed people waiting to get in them.

Giant cranes, the biggest I'd ever seen, dominated the skyline, their long swing-arms putting up girders on the frames of new hotels even as people vacationed below. We rolled by buildings with every style of architecture imaginable, their lush, manicured landscapes lit with spotlights. It was enough to make Regina gawk as if she was at Disneyland. Everything looked new and its own strange kind of wonderful so I couldn't really blame her.

For me, gild and flash wore thin real fast, but I *was* taken by heat, the earthy smell of the tropical air and the sense of the jungle waiting outside of the city; I could almost feel it, elemental and raw, barely being held in check by Cancun's concrete and stucco.

Tomacito spun through a traffic circle and pulled in front of our destination, a low rise building with a spinning spotlight out front sending beams of light that hit the skeletal frames of new high rises. People crowded underneath the silver "La Boom" sign, half them young Mexican guys in pastel suits. We got out. I leaned in the front window. Regina had already paid and tipped Tomacito but I said,

Feliz Navidad, as sincerely as I could. He smiled and said *"gracias…"* Then added *"mi amigo."*

"*Si, mi amigo*," I said.

He asked me my name.

"Dave," I said. "Short for David."

"David," he repeated. *"Daveed la barba."*

He pointed at my long hair and pulled a comic book out from the side of his seat. Conan la Barba was emblazoned on the cover above an illustration of long–haired, musclebound Conan the Barbarian.

"*Daveed la barba! Mi amigo*," Tomacito said again. *"Feliz Navidad!"*

People got in his cab. He pulled away from the curb tapping his horn to the rhythm of the song. Then he was gone. I didn't think I was going to last very long with the disco thing, but the spray of smoke and dry ice that wafted from behind the exit door when it opened looked enticing. Regina surveyed it all as if she were sizing up an algebra equation. The bouncers had separated everyone into two groups, men only and groups with women and couples. Yeah, if Regina wasn't here I'd be sunk.

"*Sombrero, señor*," asked a man sitting at the curb a few feet away.

He was weaving hats from thick green palm fronds. I was sorry I couldn't help him, he looked weary in his ragged shorts and threadbare shirt. But I only had so much money and what was I going to do with a silly hat? My mind started to spin and wonder who he was and what he was doing here. What was his life all about? What could I really do? If I thought about him for too long I wasn't going to have any fun so I forced my attention elsewhere. Four men in replicas of traditional Mexican costumes strolled through the "couples" area strumming guitars, angling for tips. Their bouncy "Feliz Navidad" was going to get old real fast but their harmony was impeccable, I had to give them that. The blank look in their eyes, distant like the bellhops at the hotel gave me a sinking feeling. For a second I thought the pudgy guy in the middle plucking the four-string looked alert and present. Maybe he was stealing looks at it all, taking in the spectacle like us. Maybe he wasn't burnt out like the rest of them. I couldn't look at him for long either.

Across the road heavy-duty floodlights illuminated the steel skeleton of a high-rise going up. Men worked on the girders high above. The sparks from their welding torches burnt out before reaching the men hauling rubble below.

"What do you think?" I asked Regina.

"I'm thinking it's going to be a chore and a half to get in," she said.

I had meant what did she think of the man with the hat and the musicians and the men working the night shift.

"I'm gonna scope it out," she said. "I'll be right back."

"I'll be right here," I said and she disappeared into the crowd around the door.

Without Regina to talk to I shifted back and forth and didn't know what to do with my hands. There were so many people and I wanted to mix it up but couldn't think of how to begin.

I looked at the door and my shoulders and calves came alive with an electric sensation. The cologne and sweat and cigarette smoke of the crowd was thicker or maybe I was just suddenly more aware of it and something else mixed in that I sensed, something like decomposing leaves and sweet, exotic florals I had no name for.

The door opened and out walked a tall girl in blue jean cut-offs and a tight shirt. The shirt was one of those black t-shirts with the white sleeves they put rock and roll iron-on's on at the mall, except hers didn't have one. She was wearing one of those palm hats from the guy at the curb and unruly dark curls stuck out in all directions from beneath it. She was the most beautiful girl I had ever seen. I couldn't look away even though she was looking right at me and was totally going to notice. She looked over her shoulder as if expecting someone to follow through the exit. Then she glanced around the crowd, smiled and walked in my direction. I guessed she was about my age but something about the confidence with which she carried herself made her seem so much older than everyone milling about, jostling for position in line and the crowd. She stopped right in front of me still smiling that amazing smile. There had to be someone behind me she was looking for.

"She your girlfriend or your sister?" she asked.

"Me?" I asked.

"Yup, you," she said. A line of acne traced the length of her jaw, tiny bumps a shade darker than her olive skin.

"My sister, yeah," I said. "How'd you know?"

"Figured she had to be from the way you're staring."

My hands reached for each other and I looked across the street at the construction.

"It's just wrong," she said.

"Sorry," I said. "I didn't mean to—"

"No, the workers," she said. "The singers. It's so wrong."

"Yeah, I was just thinking…about that…yeah exactly that," I said.

"Thought so."

"Too weird," I said. "Wait, weren't you just inside? How'd you know about Regina?"

"Don't know. Just did," she said.

She introduced herself. Her name was Anne Marie. She was from upstate, near Albany, and went to school at SUNY, where Regina did. I would have believed if she said she were from Mexico City or anywhere in Central America.

The club door opened again and three guys and a girl exited. One of the guys and the girl were tall and blond, siblings maybe. One of the other guys looked like one of the well-dressed local boys and the other I pegged as a plain old American tourist type, like me. The blond guy looked around the crowd and upon seeing Anne Marie, he beelined to us.

"This place sucks," he said with a thick accent. Something European. "Time to beach it." He held up a three quarter full bottle of tequila. "At least the bartender speaks my language."

I stood there trying to think of something funny or cool to say and I think I just said something like, "yeah." Back at school on stage behind a drum kit and a microphone I was okay but here or in any crowd I was lost.

"My friends and I were just leaving," Anne Marie said to me. "Time to move the party somewhere else."

"Yeah, cool. Nice to meet you," I said.

They sauntered away. My mind was racing. I hated that I was such an awkward dolt. Anne Marie stood there a few heartbeats longer then smiled sweetly, turned, and joined her friends.

I watched her go. I was already thinking about how I'd be thinking about her later. Wishing I had thought of something clever to say. Or that I had just said anything. I'd figure out something eventually. As a lyric. Maybe even as part of a song. All I wanted was another minute with her but what I had was a song fragment in the making. Like always.

I took a step forward. Then I darted after her.

"Hey, wait," I said and reached for her.

My hand found her shoulder. A charge ran through me. I felt like I was one of those Christmas bulbs on a string lit up for the first time. Something green appeared in my mind's eye. An egg.

The perfect, luminous green oval glowed like the moon on a cloudless night. Then it became the shape of the moon and I was watching the night sky. Something gargantuan was heading for outer space. Something that dwarfed the earth. Whatever it was I knew it was going to stop and swallow the moon whole.

"...swallow the moon," I said.

"What?" she said.

"Huh, uh I meant. Wait up, where are you all going?"

"Nowhere in particular," she said. "Any suggestions?"

"I know someplace nice. Near the water," I said.

Just then Regina emerged from the crowd.

"Looks like my little bro is a popular boy," she said, her face lit with pride.

"I was just going to sit around and do nothing all night," I said. "But then I figured we'd take my new friends to our place by the beach. Care to join us, dear sister?"

"They've got tequila, so hell yeah," she said.

Regina and I made our introductions to Anne Marie's friends and we all boisterously walked to the nearest hotel where we piled into two little green cabs. Back at our hotel the two kids from earlier were still manning the taxi stand. They gave no friendly hellos or any other sign of recognition as we passed.

We herded the group from the taxi stand to the pool area as quietly as we could, which wasn't very quiet at all. For the few moments Anne Marie had been at the hotel she had managed to pick up the few stray kids who were hanging around the pool and lobby with nothing to do and brought them into our pack. We were about a dozen now and I tried in vain to get them to keep the noise down as we headed for the dunes. The moon, higher in the sky than earlier, illuminated the rocky path that led up to the little ruin.

At the top we had a perfect vantage of the long wide beach and crashing waves. We sat in a circle inside the ruined walls, perfectly hidden from view, the glow of stars and the moon a welcome reprieve from the strip's artificial light.

The quiet stargazing lasted only a few seconds before the tequila bottle went around. The tall blond guy, Heinrich, produced a joint from his jeans pocket and passed it round as well. Our smoke wafted into the humid, salt-tinged air. The buzz of our conversation and laughter joined the roar of the sets of waves and buzz of insects and frogs.

Below on the beach a security guard's flashlight beam crossed the empty sand.

"Quiet, security is down there," Regina said.

She stuck her tongue out at me when everyone actually attempted to keep it down and leaned closer to each other to talk. Regina, Heinrich and some of the lobby refugees were getting cozy in the corner across from me with Heinrich's never ending supply of joints. The others were lining up tequila shots on the large flat stone that now served as our bar.

I moved a little closer to Anne Marie.

"So, how's Albany going," I asked her.

"I'm halfway through my freshman year. I don't look the part of a typical SUNY girl, do I," she said.

"That's a no," I said.

The bottle was passed to her and she took a swig. She tried to refrain from wincing. I got the sense it was from something more than the tequila.

"I was adopted," she said. "My mom, well, my birth mother, was from Guatemala. I'm told. You?"

She threw the question back to me so quickly I got the sense her adoption wasn't a favorite discussion topic.

"Me, I'm from New York. The suburbs. Born and raised."

"And?"

"And what?" I asked.

"And everyone's got something that makes them special," she said. "Life is short, so tell me something real, something interesting."

"I play drums and I sing. I'm in a band with some other Rochester students. But, you know, I don't have any illusions, that's why I'm in school in the first place."

"Hmmn, I bet your illusions are more interesting," she said and moved closer to me. The feel of her leg against mine was the best feeling in the world.

"I'm waiting," she said.

"For what?" I asked.

"Your illusions. Let's hear 'em. Like, why are you in the band?"

"I don't know."

"Terrible answer," she said. "Of course you know. Don't be afraid to know. I'm right here with you and I want you to tell me."

In the dark her slender leg was the same color as the rocky sand. The curve of her calf blurred out of focus as I looked past her.

"To reach people," I said.

I had never really thought about it before. Being here with her it was clear though.

"To be a light," I said. "A guide…"

She smiled.

"…to escape lives of mediocrity and all the things in this world that bring us down."

She kissed me on the cheek.

"I like that," she said. "Very much."

Everything was going great. I just wanted to keep my mouth closed before I messed it all up.

"How about you," I asked.

"I don't know," she said. "But that's okay. I'll find my place someday. I know I want to live and love and laugh and do it all. I'm in school so who knows where I'll end up or what I'll be."

"School, yeah. School got me out of town and away from my parents' never ending nags to cut my hair."

She laughed. "You here with them?"

"Yeah, them and Regina."

"I'm here with my sister and her fiancé, sorry her soon to be fiancé," she said. "My Mom's pretty conservative. The only way she'd let her go away with him was if I came along."

I was about to question the logic of that when a voice called from outside the ruin.

"Hey, who is up there?"

A flashlight shone into the ruin. A Mexican man in that ridiculous hotel uniform moved the beam back and forth to each of us, stopping on Regina who happened to be holding a joint. We were busted. My first night and the fun was over.

"Give that to me," he said, and retrieved the joint.

Nobody said anything. There was nowhere to run, no way out of the ruin but past him. I noticed the bulky radio on his belt. Was he going to call the real police?

"Don't you know this is bad for kids," he said.

He took a deep hit off it and sat down on the ground with us.

"I should know, I have four of them." He exhaled a plume of smoke. "They are safe at home in their beds so this won't hurt them."

I watched in silence as he took another hit. Then Heinrich lifted the bottle of tequila.

"Cheers to your kids, mister," he said.

Our new security guard friend introduced himself as Lucho and happily smoked Heinrich's pot and drank tequila with us giving us rambling, colorful stories full of past incidents of debauchery at the hotel.

He was in the middle of telling us some tall tale about how if you stare at the ruin and meditate you can have visions of Mayan gods when Anne Marie leaned over and whispered in my ear.

"I thought I heard a bird call from the beach," she said. "Come on."

She got up and I followed her. Lucho made a joke about us as we left but I didn't mind. Regina seemed to be hitting it off with Heinrich, which was fine by me considering what I thought of her boyfriend back home. She put her arm around him and flipped me the middle finger so he could not see when I stopped to look back.

I thought Anne Marie was going to lead me down the little hill the ruin was perched upon but she carefully walked along the ruin's outside perimeter. We turned the corner, then turned again and we were overlooking the beach.

We sat facing the ocean, our backs against the outside wall of the ruin. I could still hear the drunken stories going on only a few feet away but they were in another world.

"There," Anne Marie said, pointing to the sets of waves.

I looked and as my eyes adjusted better I made out a tall white bird wading in the tide.

"Oh, yeah," I said. I could barely concentrate. We were so close our hips were touching. She smelled of suntan lotion and sweat and tequila and pot. The night air smelled of the ocean and something tropical I couldn't place. I was so happy I was tongue-tied.

"Anne Marie is a nice name," I said.

I felt like Regina, filling the potent quiet space with chatter.

"Sweet of you to say," she said. "I hate it though."

"Well, what's in a name anyway," I said.

"A lot. Take Can-Cun. This week I learned it means serpent's nest in Mayan."

"Doesn't look like much of a serpent's nest to me."

"Not now, with all the money and jobs and all of this," she said. "I don't know what it is, local people just want to talk to me. Apparently the Yucatan's been a rebellious place for centuries. It only ceded to some semblance of law and order when the first resorts were built about ten years ago."

It sounded like something Regina might say had she given a damn about Central American history.

"Don't get me started," she said.

"Please, *get* started," I said.

She seemed pleased by that and she shifted even closer to me. Her hand found mine. I closed my fingers around hers. We sat in silence listening to the night. Our breathing. The waves. The wind. Everyone talking a few feet away. And something else, a sound, something like a lone voice in a strange language only it wasn't words, it was rhythmic. And it was lulling me. Anne Marie was so close. I reveled in her beautiful face then our lips were touching and I closed my eyes as we kissed.

The dark became green. The luminous, green egg. It trembled and a crack appeared, a thin black line spreading across its smooth surface. As pieces of shell fell away it dawned on me which of my beliefs were truth and which were illusion. There was only joy in the realization. I didn't care about all that had to be left behind.

A small triangular head, iridescent and tropical-fish green in color, poked through the hole. The baby serpent emerged, its eyes black as the dark places in the starry sky. Tongue flickering, it slithered from the egg, rose into the air, and floated above me. Above the people gathered with me and the much larger crowd gathered around us. Its flat belly scales, the bright yellow white of ripe jungle fruit, gently undulated as it hovered. Every motion had meaning. Every flick of its blue forked tongue profound. It was the answer to every question. It was purpose given form.

Wings unfolded from its back; the feathers primary reds, yellows, and blues of a rainforest bird. I reveled in their elegant shapes. I was plugged in. Lit up. Connected. To it and to everyone around me. It rose higher and higher into the starry night, growing as it ascended. It became bigger than a boa. Bigger than a car. Bigger than a plane. It blocked out the stars. I knew it was heading into outer space but first it was going to stop and swallow the moon…

—

IT WAS STARTING to get light. I hadn't realized so much time had passed. I certainly hadn't fallen asleep but I couldn't recall what I'd been thinking about or how we passed the time. Anne Marie looked at me and smiled. A sheepish expression filled her face then she beamed. I noticed the quiet; the conversation in the ruins behind us had lulled. Then Regina stuck her head through a hole in the ruin's brick wall.

"Kissy-heads. It's almost dawn. We have to get back," she said. "Dad'll be waking up soon."

"Aw, come on," I said.

"Seriously, we have to go."

A bird called from the waves below. Its cry was deep and resonant. Nothing like I had ever heard before. Regina ducked back into the ruins giving me a final moment of privacy.

"Where are you staying?" I asked.

"Not far down on the strip," Anne Marie said. "But our hotel isn't as fancy as this. You ride horses?"

"Sure," I said. But I didn't.

"Meet me tomorrow, then. At your taxi stand. Not too early, though. Let's say, the crack of noon. I'm supposed to go riding with my sister. You should come."

She got up and we both rejoined the group in the ruins. I didn't like the way Lucho was watching Anne Marie. He was talking and laughing it up but I could tell he was keeping an eye on her. Regina and Anne Marie and I said our goodbyes and left. I heard the murmur of conversation and laughter continuing on as we wound down the rocky path. The two men from earlier were unstacking the chairs and placing them around the pool. Regina and I escorted Anne Marie to the taxi stand and once she was safely on her way we slipped back into our suite.

"Wash the smell of smoke off of you," Regina said. She ushered me into the bathroom and squirted a dash of perfume in my hair.

"Drink water and take some of these. You'll thank me later." She handed me two aspirin from her toiletry bag.

THE SERPENT'S SHADOW

"Remember this next time you think you know how many intelligent cells are in my body," she said.

A few minutes later I lay on the fold-out couch, replaying it all, my parents snoring in the bedroom. I pictured Anne Marie emerging from the club, her dark curls sticking out from that hat. I imagined the line of her jaw and her full lips from my vantage next to her on the ruin. My tired mind drifted to images of the cab driver, the men singing, the men cleaning the pools and I couldn't force them away. What a strange cosmic twist of fate that these people should be singing for their supper in such a way. Anne Marie understood this. Perhaps wishes of the people here were not as strong as others, the force of their collective will not able to withstand that of those who came after them. Conquistadors. Governments. Foreign corporations. I wanted to go back out. To watch that bird in the waves with Anne Marie as the sun came up. An image of her and me standing in a road flanked by jungle flashed into my mind. Our hands were linked. I knew I was drunk and high and tired. I felt like one of those flashing light bulbs that had been going all night and I just let myself wink out.

2.

"RISE AND SHINE, sleepy heads," Dad said.

I still felt drunk and spinny and tried to ignore him.

"Come on. I don't want to waste a minute. I've got something special planned for you. Into your bathing suits."

I opened my eyes. The little clock on the table said six thirty. I'd been asleep maybe an hour, tops.

There was no escaping him. His mind was set. I changed. Mom and Dad had prepared a makeshift breakfast on the terrace of airplane peanuts and some juice and muffins.

"Bring lotion, we're going on a boat," Mom said.

I loved the way Hawaiian Tropic smelled. Maybe it would wake me up.

As we walked to the taxi stand, looking like another typical family on vacation, I glanced at the ruin for some sign our friends were still there. I heard only the sound of the waves and wind and the early going tourists, like us, preparing for the day. On the lawn gray iguanas were crawling out of holes and onto perches on the rocks to catch the early morning sun.

We took a cab to a marina and of course *Feliz Navidad* jangled from the tinny radio. The cab looked immaculate but smelled of pine disinfectant masking something rancid, no doubt a remnant of the past night's debauchery. I jumped out the second we arrived at the "marina", a single dock, an equipment shack, and some plastic tables and chairs clustered by the shore. Even here strings of green lights wrapped around the palms like vines with dormant, nocturnal flowers.

A white sailboat bobbed in the water next to the dock. I put my fake raybans on and climbed onto a spot on the bow as everyone else, about a dozen other passengers, got on. An engine sputtered to life and we motored out into the bay. Mom and Dad snapped pictures and I ignored their directions to smile. I kept my eyes closed beneath my shades. The boat sped faster and faster until it was bouncing over the small waves so fast I felt I might lose my balance. I opened my eyes. We were cutting across a watery plane of intense bright blue. Cool salt spray whipped my face. The wind blew my hair. It tasted clean. Cleaner than that first mild day at the end of winter when you know spring is right around the corner. We raced to nowhere, the sky blue horizon blurring with the unreal, clear, sun-shimmering water.

The engine slowed and the boat circled. We seemed to be zeroing in on a location. The glass-transparent water allowed a perfect view of the micro cities of bulbous white coral formations below. I was still slightly drunk and slightly high, but this was no longer a problem. I wondered if maybe Mom had brought along some of those airplane peanuts. Mom and Dad and even Regina too were staring out into the ocean. They'd never seen the Caribbean before. And neither had I. Sailing the Caribbean Seas was something Dad had always said he would do. I guessed their dazed-out look, the look of being immersed in such blue for the first time, was the one that matched how I felt. I liked it.

We spent the morning snorkeling. From out here, Cancun and its big hotel strip was a glistening stretch of white on the shore. To its South was nothing but miles and miles of beach and green as far as I could see. I pictured what the scene would look like without the strip, just Cancun, the serpent's nest, like Anne Marie had told me.

After all the snorkelers were back on board we switched to sails for the return journey. From the stern came a fluttering sound that reminded me of playing cards in the spokes of a child's bicycle. Glittering silver fish glided above the waves, returning to the water with hundreds of tiny splashes. I had worried the trip was going to suck but my fears had been put to rest. I was really happy to be alive.

ON THE RIDE back I noticed the areas of terrible poverty we had driven through. Children in rags chased our cab as it passed. I was so tired and the images so disturbing I just closed my eyes. Back at the hotel Regina hugged Dad and thanked him. I didn't moan and groan when Mom gave the camera to the bellhop to take family pictures of us in the hotel lobby.

I took a really fast shower, changed into a t-shirt, cutoffs, and the sturdy running sneakers I had worn on the plane down.

"Lunch time," Dad said.

"I was thinking we could walk the beach and go have lunch at one of the neighboring hotels," Mom said.

"No, I'm going to stay here. Explore around for a while," I said.

Regina gave a mischievous smile, and mouthed, "Have fun" to me.

"I'm going to read and maybe nap on the beach," she said. "I didn't sleep so much last night."

"You kids. Your parents are putting you to shame," Dad said.

ANNE MARIE WAS waiting by the taxi stand. I loved the way the sun was hitting her jet black hair. A young couple I took to be her sister and her sister's fiancé-to-be were impatiently standing next to her.

"You sleep well?" she asked.

"Don't ask," I said. "You?"

"Wild dreams, but besides that, like a baby. Ready to ride?"

"Sure," I said.

She introduced me to her sister, Trudy and Reginald. Reginald wore a white cowboy hat, jeans, and a plaid shirt.

"Pleased to meet you," he said. Though I didn't get the sense he was.

A cab raced out of the waiting area, out of turn, and pulled up to us. Tomacito!

"Feliz Navidad," Tomacito said.

"You know him?" Anne Marie asked.

"My name is Tomacito. *Mucho gusto*," Tomacito said to her. "He and his sister are my friends."

I noticed the *Conan la Barba* comic tucked between the seat and the armrest. Tomacito's round face looked young enough to still enjoy the comic, but his eyes reminded me of Dad's. Eyes that were used to watching a family and were eager to please, eager to do a day's work for a day's wage.

We got in. Reginald told him where we were going, a ranch called Alfonso's. We pulled onto the strip and headed south.

"I've been riding at Alfonso's since I was a kid," Reginald said. "My dad imported some of the best horses at our ranch from him. It's going to be a special day for us, honey," he said to Trudy.

Trudy blushed and smiled. I guessed the whole engagement thing wasn't such a secret.

Just past the airport the paved road changed to packed dirt. A few minutes later we passed what Tomacito said were Mayan ruins but looked like non-descript piles of rubble rising from the scrub and growth. Thousands of gray iguanas rested on the sun-bleached gray stones and on each other, taking in the sun. The scrub and trees on both sides of the road became thicker a few minutes later. We had hit the edge of the jungle. Then for miles and miles there was nothing but green.

At some point we passed a man holding the biggest gun I'd ever seen, just standing there, at attention, on the side of the road in the middle of nowhere.

"What is he doing?" I asked.

"Guarding a trail into the jungle," Tomacito said.

"Why," I asked. "Drugs?"

"Protecting the archeology, maybe," Anne Marie said.

"That's a pretty big gun," Reginald said. "I wouldn't be so sure he isn't a looter protecting his claim."

"How can you tell?" I asked Tomacito.

"You cannot. Better not to know," he said. "The Yucatan is a land at war."

"War? Here?" I asked.

Tomacito seemed surprised. I wasn't sure if it was from the question or that I asked it.

"Yes here. There is fighting here that history has forgotten."

"You mean never heard of," Reginald said. "Which side are you on?"

This question seemed to bother Tomacito even more.

"I'm on the side of my family. I work hard for my family. I'm on that side."

We sped through a small village. It wasn't much. A few sad-looking children watched as we passed. I took his answer as a cue to change the subject.

"You ever been to the city? New York." I asked Anne Marie.

"We didn't care so much for New York City," Reginald said. "You like it?"

His question sounded more like an accusation. I wasn't going to
get a minute in with her with him around.

"The three of us went a few years ago," Anne Marie said. "Trudy
had a modeling offer. Mom wouldn't let her go, of course, unless I
came along."

"Must have been a blast," I said.

"I grew up with the notion the city was romantic," she said. "But—"

A grimace overcame her face.

"To put it mildly. It's a concrete jungle," she said. "A rat race."

"Right," I said.

"You don't know much Marley, do you?"

I was going to try and convince her that I did but wasn't fast
enough.

"Oh, you're missing out," she said. "Don't worry, I'll school you."

"Ever ride a horse, David?" Reginald asked.

"Sure," I said. He didn't need to know I could count the number
of times on one hand.

"Oh, got many horses in New York City?"

"No," I said.

"Don't worry. I'll school ya," he said, mocking Anne Marie.

We drove another half hour, flanked by endless green. Tomacito
turned onto a smaller road so obscured by the trees I didn't see it
till we were upon it. The road headed into the swath of jungle in
between the road and the shore and became smaller and bumpier
with each turn. The last bit of it was lined with sun-bleached white
conch shells. The jungle at its edges seemed manicured with fruit
trees and flowering bushes.

Tomacito stopped the car. Reginald paid and arranged for him
to return for us an hour before dark.

Fresh salt air blowing over the jungle's earthy reek greeted us as
Tomacito drove away. A path lined with shells, just like the road, led
to a house where it forked off to a stable.

THE SERPENT'S SHADOW

Beneath some of the flowered trees not far off the path laid over-turned stone tablets. Mayan faces were carved into them. Wax and candle stubs formed colorful collages on their tops. One had freshly cut orchids and a bundle of incense sticks burning at its base.

I wanted to stop and look, but a thin Mayan man walked out of the house to greet us. Long, stringy hair flowed from beneath his dirty white cowboy hat. He wore heavy jeans and black leather boots despite the heat.

"Welcome to Alfonso's Ranch," he said and smiled proudly.

He was missing a few teeth and his skin was dry and scarred.

"We're a bit short staffed today so your horses are not yet ready. Please, walk over that way, the path leads to the beach. Relax. Pick some fruit and take photos while you wait."

The hand painted sign over the path read Welcome to Alfonso's. The words *Alfonso's* was crossed out and a triangle with a swiggle through it was painted over it in green.

Reginald shook Ramon's hand then the two men hugged. The embrace was awkward, I thought, as if it were a last minute decision and not a natural outpouring of affection.

"I remember when you were just a little cowboy," Ramon said. "Look how you've grown."

I wasn't convinced Reginald actually recognized the guy.

"Yeah, and look at how much Cancun has grown," Reginald said. "Last time I was here it was just a fishing village. Now the whole coast is going to be one big resort."

"I hope not," Ramon said. "Where will we take the tourists riding then?"

Reginald chewed his tobacco.

"Alfonso always dreamed of building a big resort. I'm sure he'd find a way. Where is the old man?"

"He could not be here today," Ramon said. "He is with his family for Christmas Eve."

Reginald didn't blink.

"Back in the day Dad and I and the family had our Christmas dinner here. I thought he was going to surprise us with a big dinner and the whole family waiting..."

"Don't worry," Ramon said. "Do not worry. Everything is fine. We've been expecting you and your day will go as planned. Everything is going as planned..."

Trudy became excited.

"Pick me a fast horse, Honey," Trudy said.

She took Reginald by the hand and started for the beach. Reginald let her pull as he stood there. He turned toward me and spit tobacco, his face part disinterest part dirty look. Then he let Trudy lead him.

I asked Anne Marie if she'd be all right for a second. She replied in a thick mock-drawl and said she would so long as I picked her a fast horse. I had to use the bathroom and while I was at it I was going to get a better look at those gravestone-looking things along the path.

I walked along the stables peering in at the horses. Around back was an empty slot full of hay. To my surprise, poking out from a behind a bale was someone's leg. I thought someone was taking a nap or goofing off and that I should just leave. I thought about just going out back, in the jungle, but with those stones out there I figured that was probably a big no-no.

"*Donde el bano?*" I asked, with a cough.

I received no answer so I repeated myself and walked over. The bale shifted. A body clunked to the floor. The guy was stiff, his neck purple and puffy. I turned to run and crashed into Ramon who was standing in the stable's entrance.

"Holy shit, Ramon!" I said. "I was just looking for the bathroom and then—"

"It's okay," Ramon said, all slow. "He was on the trail this morning, and how do you say it in English? *Fur de Lance?* No, that's

THE SERPENT'S SHADOW

French. Is it the same? The serpent got him. It was his time. It's a hard life we have living with the jungle."

I looked at the dead man, his swollen neck plump as a melon.

"We have to carry on. It's my job to take you riding now. Our family is depending on it."

I'd never seen a dead body before. This guy probably just wanted to make a living, like my dad, but instead of job sites and sawdust and foul-mouthed job supers and clients, he had to brave the jungle.

"Holy shit? Is that Alfonso? We're in the middle of nowhere. What do we do? Do we call an ambulance? Is there a phone?"

"Calm down. Stay calm my friend. We are not in the middle of nowhere. And everything is as it should be. His family knows. And will come. Arrangements are made. No reason for the family to lose a big job and customer too."

"I don't know," I said. "Maybe we shouldn't go today."

"I'm sorry it upset you. If you are scared and want to go I can send someone to call for a ride."

"I'm going to see what Reginald thinks."

"Today is supposed to be their special day," Ramon said. "He made arrangements for a picnic on the beach to propose today. He's all paid. I'd hate to ruin all that."

"Um, I don't know," I said. "I mean. Holy shit!"

"Holy shit, yes," he said and he laughed. "And what else do you say? Shit happens? Life is tough."

"You don't even look upset," I said. "What am I supposed to do? Just go out there and pretend to have a good time?"

He re-covered poor Alfonso with hay.

"No. Go out there and have a good time. Do not pretend. Whatever you do it will not change things here. If you want to leave there is a phone a few miles up the road. We can arrange to take you there. If you stay while they are on their picnic I will show you the jungle. It will be the best day of your life."

39

I didn't want to ruin everything. I was shaken up. Anne Marie wanted this. I still wanted to go. With her.

"Uh, I don't know. Let's just go, I guess," I said.

"Very good," he said.

"Can you do me a favor?" I asked. "I'm really not such a good rider."

Ramon went to the next stall and led a magnificent black horse out.

"A guy like you, I'm sure you ride just fine," he said. "Come on, let's get you in the saddle."

I remembered once asking Dad how he had moved on. About how he had gotten through the rough stuff in his life. The stuff he didn't often talk about. When he was a kid and had come to the US after the war. I had gotten into yet another fight at school or something. I don't remember what. I only remember what he had said. "Sometimes you have to just pretend things are alright. And one day, maybe if you are lucky things will actually start to be alright. Or at least feel that way."

I guess that's what Dad had done. Did he go to work and come home and laugh around with us and do everything even when things were not alright? I guess he had no choice but to pretend. Or if he had a choice it was a selfless one. I figured I could make Ramon take us back. Part of me wanted to. But then there would be no ride in the jungle. No time with Anne Marie. I thought of Dad laughing with Regina and me. I hated pretending.

3.

I PUT MY foot in the stirrup and with a boost from Ramon I was up in the saddle feeling precariously high above the world. My horse snorted with a shake and clomped to the house where the others were waiting, as if he knew the drill. I grabbed the saddle horn and tried to look comfortable. After a moment, Ramon followed leading three horses and saddled everyone up.

I waved to Anne Marie and she made like she was holding a camera with her fingers and pretended to take my picture.

Neither of us had a camera, but it didn't matter. This was a place I knew I would coming back to. All this pristine beauty. This was what was real. This was what was missing from my life.

"A fast one. Tell him I want a fast one," Trudy said to Reginald as if Ramon was not there.

"I want a fast one, too," Anne Marie said, mocking her sister. Though I knew she was serious.

She patted my horse's snout.

"What's his name?" she asked.

"Diablo," Ramon said. "Because she can run like the devil."

Everyone laughed. Ramon looked confused. I don't think he had meant to make a joke.

"Deep thoughts?" Anne Marie said. "You're on vacation. Try not to look so serious. Smile."

I made a cheesy grin and pretended to pose for a picture. Two dogs that had been laying in the shade of the porch stood up and stretched. They were dirty but they looked happy and it struck me they were living the good life doing whatever they wanted to do, hanging around in the jungle all day. Ramon galloped over from the stables on a mottled brown and white stallion. He led us onto the path to the beach, the dogs flanking us in the brush.

"Look, they're herding us," Anne Marie said.

I got the sense they were guarding against snakes, but I said nothing and managed to keep my smile.

We emerged onto pristine white sand, the water's edge about a hundred yards away. A dozen shades of turquoise stretched to where the horizon disappeared in a sparkling line of white. No beach back home was like this. There was nothing but clean, clean sand. This was how beaches were supposed to be.

"A beautiful day. Right amigos?" Ramon said.

He had read my mind. It was a beautiful day. I told myself everything was going to be great. Except for Reginald and Trudy being with us, everything was great, and soon we were going to leave them behind.

The horses walked in a line on the wet sand at the water's edge, the tide gently ebbing and flowing over their hoofs. Little birds with stick-like legs and beaks that looked too big for their bodies ran ahead of us picking at what the water left. A pair of pelicans floated in the shallows between the shore and where the waves were breaking about twenty yards away.

Anne Marie gave her horse a little kick and she took off in a gallop. Trudy followed, leaving me with Ramon and Reginald who wasted no time in lighting up a cigar.

"Guy like you back in town who sold it to me says it's a Cuban," he said to Ramon.

THE SERPENT'S SHADOW

The thing was fouling up the air even worse than him, I thought.

Reginald reached inside his front pants pocket and produced a diamond ring. He held it up for us to see. The small gem glinted in the sunlight.

"Today's the big day," he said. "Alfonso said everything was ready."

"Yes, señor," Ramon said. "Everything is ready as planned and waiting for you farther up the beach."

"Alfonso said he'd make sure we have some, ya know...privacy."

"No problem," Ramon said. "I will take care of the *chico* and *chica* and you will have the beach to yourself."

Reginald put the ring back in his pocket, maneuvered his horse next to Ramon and clapped him on the back.

"You're a hell of a guy Ray-mon," he said. He kicked his horse and set off after Trudy.

The horse Ramon had given him was older and struggled to catch up to the girls. Ramon smiled when I laughed. Up ahead Anne Marie galloped in the shallows, her sister not far behind.

"So graceful. Like a princess," Ramon said. "She was raised in the fourth world, like you, but it is like she never left her home."

The fourth world? Was that what he meant by back home?

He had no idea Anne Marie was from Guatemala, but I wasn't going to get into it with him. I didn't like the spaced-out look on his face when he spoke.

"You are a child of the fourth world too," he said. "Yet you appreciate all this. How is that?"

"Come on? How could you not," I said. "Even Mister and Missus America to be over there get it."

"You understand what they do not," Ramon said. "Even fools can see the wonder but you see the importance. You see that this our home. And you see the struggle of our people."

I don't know how he got all that from me, but it was true. I liked that he knew that I got it.

"Aw, Ramon how bad can it be? You live here."

For a second I thought I had angered him. There was something going on with him. But I couldn't get a read.

"I see why you say that," he said. "The sun. The waves. The jungle. Life is hard for Mayan people. We are strong and not afraid of work but yes life is hard when everyone tries to take from you."

He didn't look at me when he spoke and I got the sense he was talking to himself as much as he was to me.

"Come," he said. "I want to show you this."

He led me across the beach to the edge of the jungle. A cluster of bees had gathered on a coconut that had fallen from one of the palms. They were much smaller than the bees back home, each barely the size of a housefly. More of them flew back and forth from the coconut to the jungle.

"Mayan bees," Ramon said. "They are like us Mayans. Hard working. Easy going. And they work together. Do you see? They have no sting. They labor and labor and make the sweetest honey but have no sting to fight and protect it."

I thought of Dad. He was the hardest working person I knew. And the smartest. He knew how to build houses and could fix anything. But when a customer refused to pay him, he was stuck and did nothing. It was like he was born without a sting too. It wasn't fair.

"Nature can be cruel," I said.

"Yes," Ramon said. "Yes you see it."

I couldn't decide which was worse, when he looked all spaced out and far away or when he was lit up and intensely focused on me.

"Nature *is* cruel," he said. "Life is not fair. How do you Americans say? This is the story of my life. Listen, and I tell you the story of our history. The Spanish came to take from us. The Mexican Government came to take from us. Everyone takes from the Mayan people. They kill us. They kill each other. For treasure…for our *true* treasure. This land. This beautiful land."

THE SERPENT'S SHADOW

I watched the bees gathering moisture from droplets of coconut water. Only when one bee landed did another take to the air and fly away.

"All Mexicans are not the same," Ramon said. "I want you to know that I am not really Mexican. I am Mayan."

He didn't look it. He did have dark eyes and dark hair but he was taller than Tomacito and his face was a mix of all sorts of features.

"Many times we Mayans revolted against Mexico. Did you know that? My grandfather fought them here in these very jungles. They killed our people. Burned our homes. Stole from us. And now they have done worse. They put the city and hotel strip where Cancun used to be. Rich people from all over the world parade around. They seduce our children with the Rolling Stones. MTV. Pac-Man. Sports Illustrated girls. It's all shit. All the wealth and promises...it really is just shit...and illusions. Still, my son wants to leave our village and go the hotel zone to work as soon as he is able..."

He stopped in the middle of that last bit; that faraway look had come over him again. Maybe it was too painful, too close to home, I thought. After a second I realized he was watching Anne Marie.

"She is special," he said. "It is a blessing that she desires you. Do you understand?"

"Me?" I said.

I was doing everything I could not to blow it with her. I was glad he chalked me up as okay. Odd as he was some of what he was saying made sense and I was glad he didn't put me in the same box as Reginald and Trudy and people like them.

"What are you waiting for? Go to her," Ramon said.

"I can't ride," I said.

He laughed. Then muttered something under his breath. Diablo broke into a gallop.

The dogs took off too and ran alongside. I held on for dear life and gripped the saddle with my legs. Diablo splashed through the water. I yelled stop. And whoa. And a couple of things in Spanish but she wouldn't listen. I wasn't riding, I was being taken for a ride and I felt every jolt.

I heard the scrape of hoofs hitting stone. Diablo slipped and skidded sideways. She reared, scaring the little shore birds into flight. I thought I was going to fall but somehow managed to hold on.

After a few seconds of neighing and flailing her front legs, Diablo settled down with a snort and walked back and forth nervously in the mud. I listened to my heart beat and the sound of the ocean lapping the shore. The birds landed a short distance away and resumed their high pitched twit, twit, twits and scavenging. I watched Anne Marie disappear around the bend about a hundred yards up.

A pelican descended from the sky above the waves, and passed right over me. It glided over the beach leaving a wake in the air behind it as if it were sailing through molten glass. Where there was nothing seconds ago I saw buildings. Structures of molded concrete and glass. Glistening blue swimming pools. As far as I could see were buildings, buildings, buildings crowding the shore. I gagged. They were more than ugly. They were just wrong. A terrible sound devoured the stillness. Blaring music. The roar of a plane. The miasma of lots and lots of people. I saw what I thought was my Dad driving down the tropical highway. But it was me. A much older me. A shadow passed across the moon. Diablo reared again. I struggled to hold on but she bucked me. I landed face down on the hard packed mud. I gasped for breath. Everything became blurry and distorted. I laid there sucking air and at some point the gentle sound of the water and stillness returned. The beach again was nothing but white sand framed by the horizon and the wall of jungle.

I rolled onto my back and let the pain in my stomach subside. My hands sunk into the mud. Beneath was solid rock. I dug around a bit and uncovered a flat stone. It looked ancient like one of the ones from the little temple at our hotel. Anne Marie and Ramon must have seen me fall and were trotting over. Diablo sloshed through the shallows and stood next to Ramon's horse as if nothing had happened.

"Amigo, you held on like a champion," Ramon said.

"This is the hardest beach ever," I said. "There are stones everywhere."

Ramon hopped off his horse and cleared away some more mud.

"Yes, you noticed," he said. "This is *sac be*. Sorry the words are Mayan. They mean white road. This is one of the white roads. An ancient Mayan highway."

Anne Marie arrived and asked if I was okay.

"Yeah" I said. "Just got the wind knocked out of me. I'll be fine. I'm seeing stars though. And something weird."

That got Ramon's attention.

"You saw something, amigo?"

"I don't know," I said and sat up.

"Please, tell me," Ramon said.

"It happened so quick. There was a bird. Everything got blurry. There were a lot of buildings."

"You had a vision," he said.

"I don't know. I guess."

"You are on a white road. And you've had a vision," he said.

He looked so pleased.

"I must tell you the Mayan world is all connected," he said. "The white roads connect everything. They are everywhere here. Beneath this beach. Beneath the jungle. Connecting all our ancient cities. All the pyramids. Even the ones the fourth world doesn't know about. And probably ones we Mayans do not know."

This had him really excited. With his finger he drew two big triangles in the mud and a few smaller ones. Then he drew lines between them.

"This is the Mayan world," he said. He pointed to one of the large triangles. "This is Chi-Chen-Itza. The big pyramid here in the

Yucatan. Tikal is there in Guatemala. They are the big cities. The excavated ones you probably have seen."

"I was born in Guatemala," Anne Marie said. "My adopted Mom said I was from a town near Tikal."

I thought Ramon was going to explode with joy.

"Tikal is the ancient Mayan capitol," he said. "It all makes sense now. I see. I see why you two were brought to me."

Anne Marie and I looked at each other and smiled. I stifled a laugh. We were brought to him because Reginald wanted to get married and Anne Marie loved horses.

"The beautiful thing you will see is that it is not only our cities, all Mayans are connected too. Come, come," he said. "The sun is high. And I promised you a special day."

"Wait. What about Trudy?" Anne Marie said.

Ramon pointed behind us. On the beach in the distance Trudy and Reginald sat on a bright striped blanket with a picnic basket.

"Today is their special day," Ramon said.

I pretended to gag myself with my finger in my mouth.

"Sorry," I said.

"Don't be," Anne Marie said. "I'm happy to be away from them."

"They will be okay," Ramon said. "And will be right there when we return."

He helped me back on Diablo and we trotted to a patch of palms at the edge of the jungle. Ramon dismounted his horse and placed his saddlebag on the sand. He wrapped his legs around a palm trunk and pulled himself up with his arms. At the top he threw down three ripe coconuts then slid down. He took a machete and a brown bottle from his bag and opened the coconuts with a swift chop to the top of each one.

He poured golden liquid from the bottle into each of the coconuts and handed one to Anne Marie and one to me.

"Xtabentun," he said. "Honey liquor. Made by Mayans with honey from Mayan bees."

THE SERPENT'S SHADOW

It tasted sweet, like honey mixed in with the coconut water with a kick of something spicy and that sort of tasted like licorice. The first swallow felt warm in my throat.

"It is made with flowers which are called xtabentun, too. In English you say Christmas vine. My grandfather called it snake vine. There is some, there," he said and pointed to a vine with white flowers entwined in the brush on the path ahead. They looked like big white morning glories.

"Drink the rest as we ride," he said.

He got back onto his horse and set off on the trail into the jungle. Anne Marie went next and I followed. The trees and vines were thicker than at the ranch but the narrow trail was well maintained.

I saw something move up ahead. A person and then another walked across the trail.

"I just saw someone," I said.

Diablo neighed.

"Easy, devil horse," I said.

"Yes, there are people living here," Ramon said. "There is a village not far away. About forty families. They have everything they need from the jungle."

We trotted to where they crossed the trail but there was no one there. A small stela, like the ones at the ranch, stood in the brush. The stone was old but it had been cleaned and I could see the carving very clearly; it looked like a warrior in profile surrounded by Mayan glyphs. He wore an elaborate head dress. Lines of what I knew from class was supposed to be smoke were coming out of his nose and mouth. The smoke above him turned into the body of a snake.

Atop the stela was a lit candle resting in a nook made from layers of melted wax.

"It's beautiful," Anne Marie said.

"He is a Mayan priest," Ramon said. "He is having a vision and talking to the gods. Look at this one."

We moved up the trail and stopped at another stela. The carving was of a woman facing front. She wore long robes, had a skull for a face, and held a scythe. The stone was clean and barely weathered. What looked like fresh red paint dripped from the scythe's blade.

"Sante Muerte," Ramon said. "La Señora de las Sombres. She is Saint Death. The Lady of Shadows. Some call her the White Lady."

"It isn't old like the rest, why?" Anne Marie asked.

"Many worship the White Lady," Ramon said. "Now, even more than ever. It is believed she grants miracles. The families that live here know beneath this trail is a white road so they put it here with the others. Come, I want to show you where the road goes."

The trail opened into a clearing where the canopy was thinner. We stopped and Ramon tied the horses to a tree in the shade. There was a filled water trough waiting. Ramon took his saddlebag and slung it over his shoulder.

"The rest of the way is on foot," he said.

The path continued on the other side of the clearing. Fruit trees and conch shells lined the well-worn trail. Every dozen yards or so was a stela. It was amazing how many there were.

We turned a bend and came across a group of women kneeling before a stela with *xtabentun* vines growing on it. The women rose when they saw us and silently walked into the jungle in a line. One of them was wearing a pink hotel uniform. The stela they had been kneeling in front of had been freshly painted. The carved figure and glyphs were adorned with bright primary colors.

There was another woman at the next stela on the trail. She was painting the carving with a stick and paint from a rusty metal can. She looked at Ramon as we passed but otherwise paid us no mind.

I wanted to talk to Anne Marie alone, to tell her how amazing all of this was. How my teacher was wrong about Mayan being a dead language and religion but Ramon was too close and she was captivated by everything. The stelae. The people we passed. And also

Ramon. He knew everything about the jungle and she was hanging on his every word.

He pointed out different plants and herbs. More *xtabentun*. Lemongrass. Some with odd names like billyweed and gumbo limbo.

"This one don't touch," he said pointing to a tree with reddish brown bark.

"It will give you a rash. Like poison ivy," he said. "But the cure is never far away."

He touched a green tree trunk with small spikes growing from it a few feet behind the reddish tree.

"This one is the cure," he said. "See? The jungle gives us all we need," he said. "We should give *it* what *it* needs."

"What could the jungle possibly need from us?" Anne Marie said.

Ramon thought about it. He didn't have an easy answer waiting. He paced in the brush for a moment then said, "Come here."

He led us to a big tree wrapped in vines.

"Look," he said. "Third branch up, second fork over."

I followed the trunk up into the canopy and tried to figure out where he was pointing.

"Yes, there, stop," he said to Anne Marie.

"Oh, I see it. A snake," she said.

I realized I was looking at it too. A green snake about three inches thick wrapped around a fork in the branches in a tight knot, its shiny skin a shade lighter than the emerald green leaves.

Ramon pointed again and again showing us locations of other snakes in the branches of surrounding trees.

"They are young tree boas," he said. "See how perfectly they fit in with the trees? They sleep during the day and in the evening they come down to feed."

He stood silent with his head craned up.

"There is nothing more beautiful than watching them wind down the tree trunks as the sun comes down," he said. "To answer your question, chica, they need what the jungle needs. To be left in peace. They don't need us. All they need, they have here. This place is their place. Left alone they will hunt and live and breed and thrive. Why don't people see that?"

He turned and faced Anne Marie and me.

"I don't know," she said.

I didn't know either. Maybe I had been in the jungle too long. Ramon was making sense.

"We're almost here," he said.

The path led into thicker jungle. The humidity carried the scent of moist earth. I couldn't shake the feeling I was being watched. Were there more snakes in these trees? The people we had seen were probably nearby and I knew there were many other things hiding in the dense foliage. I realized the two dogs were gone, and just when I wanted to see them most.

A group of Mayans were walking on the trail ahead of us. They stopped and silently watched us pass. They were young. Their clothes looked like mismatched hand-me-downs. Old track shorts. An out of style polo shirt. One wore a Rolling Stones tour jersey. I'm sure Ramon loved that. Why were they so quiet? Surely they knew Ramon. After we passed they walked off the trail into the jungle. The trail turned right and I caught a glimpse of them. It looked like they were clearing the undergrowth off a mound of dirt and rubble.

We walked a few minutes more and came upon a man standing in the path holding a gun. The guy was Dad's age. His face was weathered and his eyes looked tired. He had on a pair of surfing shorts that had gone out of style back home years ago and a t-shirt with the Corona beer logo on it. He held a rifle with both his hands. It looked old and worn to me but from the way he held it I got the sense it could still fire.

The man and Ramon exchanged a few words in Mayan and Ramon ushered us past him into another clearing, this one about the size of half a football field. At first I thought he had brought us to a huge mound of rubble as tall as the trees but then I realized the gargantuan mass of dirt and vines and saplings was a pyramid. A huge, unexcavated pyramid. It looked nothing like the glistening images of the ones on the airport posters and flyers in the hotel lobby. Steep steps leading up the middle had been cleared. Pieces of carved stone in the few cleared areas next to the steps were visible. The rest remained in the jungle's grasp.

At the top was a structure about a few yards square. It bore the signs and stains of having been cleared of growth but a few vines had made their way back and grew on its stone walls. A rectangular opening a few feet high was in the center of the wall facing us.

"Wow," Anne Marie said.

"Wow, right," I said.

"It is impressive, yes," Ramon said.

"I've never seen a pyramid before," Anne Marie said.

"Neither have I," I said.

"It is not just a pyramid," Ramon said. "It is a calendar. A very sophisticated calendar that uses a very precise method of measuring time. All Mayan buildings have purposes. They were built with a precision that cannot be matched, even today with modern machines."

"Right, right," I said. "I learned about this."

"Very good," Ramon said to me as if he was praising a child. "And do you know what day is today?"

"My last day of vacation?" Anne Marie said. "My birthday?"

"Christmas," I said.

He shook his head. "Today is the solstice. The winter solstice. The shortest day of the year."

The canopy rustled with movement. A group of monkeys were swinging above passing across the clearing. Twirling leaves fell in their wake. I felt very small seeing their thin black forms navigate the tree tops. I didn't feel like I was doing some tourist thing anymore. I was in the real world. The real jungle. And it terrified me. These were real monkeys. And real Mayan people. Everything was much stranger than I could have imagined. I'd seen real guns. And a dead body. Someone had gotten hurt. This was living without a net. I was small. I was vulnerable. I reached for Anne Marie's hand. She closed it around mine. Ramon noticed and smiled.

"On this pyramid and those like it are carvings of great serpents descending from the top. You can see part of one there next to the stairs."

We had moved outside of the protection of the leaves and branches that were shielding us from the sun. I really felt the heat.

"Each level of the pyramid represents a unit of time. This pyramid is precisely positioned so when the solstice begins the shadow of the serpent moves down the pyramid and reaches the ground, where the stone head is, at the moment of the solstice."

Most of the growth had been removed from the clearing's floor. We had stepped onto the ancient, weather pitted stones of a *sac be*. The road ended at the base of the pyramid where the stairs began.

"My ancestors did all this without any modern tools. They were masters of building. And math and science and so much more," Ramon said. "They kept their knowledge in great books which were handed down from generation to generation. When the Spanish came to conquer us they sought out all our books and destroyed them."

"Except for the Dresden Codex," I said. "And a few others. I learned about this too."

"Yes," Ramon said. "Only a few codices remain."

He pronounced codices strangely as if the sound of it had a bitter taste.

"It was a great tragedy," he said. "They were so easy to find. So easy to take. The codices were kept in the pyramid tops. Now what is left of our great knowledge is in museums in the fourth world... Paris. Dresden. Madrid..."

That faraway look came over him again. He clutched his saddlebag.

"I will show you what I can. At Chi-Chen-Itza the pyramid has been restored. You can see all the levels of the calendar there and see the great serpents, heads and all. Many visitors are gathered there right now to watch the shadows descend. That's what the serpent has come to mean for many people. A tourist show. It means much more to me. What does it mean to you?"

I shrugged.

"To me it means throwing away the old," Anne Marie said. "Shedding skin."

Ramon clapped and Anne Marie beamed. Ramon looked at me to see if I would try again to answer. Again I shrugged.

"Come, now we will climb," he said.

He walked on the *sac be* to the pyramid and climbed up the first steps using his hands to hold on. He reached a gap in the stone stairs about a few yards up where there was only rubble and gravel and he had to pull himself up.

"Come on," he said and extended his hand. "What are you two waiting for?"

Anne Marie and I smiled at each other and raced to him. She beat me to the pyramid and began climbing first. I followed. The stairs were steeper than they looked and I had no choice but to use my hands like Ramon did.

Anne Marie reached the gap and took hold of Ramon's hand. She pivoted to me and extended her other arm to me.

"Come on," she said. "We'll pull you up."

I reached for her. As my hand closed around hers the jungle went silent. The din of the birds, the insects, the rustle of trees and plants was replaced with a steady thump which I realized was the sound of my heart...and Anne Marie's heart...and Ramon's.

My hand, my arm, my whole body was alive with energy. I felt every inch of Anne Marie's hand around mine and every inch of Ramon's around hers. Anne Marie's excitement and Ramon's strange, nervous joy bloomed inside me as if the feelings were my own. A connection had been made. A circuit had been closed and something was flowing through us.

The world flashed green. Bright primary colors exploded in my mind's eye. Reds and yellows and blues. I was seeing Anne Marie and Ramon before me but I was also looking out to the jungle. I saw the white roads beneath it all leading from the pyramid through the trees. Only I wasn't seeing it with my eyes at all. Some other sense had kicked in. I was feeling the white road. I sensed its shape and size and location. I felt Ramon and Anne Marie's gaze upon me and I knew there were people in the jungle around us and on the white road. But not because I had seen them earlier. I felt them watching. They were watching the pyramid. Watching us. I knew their hands were linked, like ours.

I slipped backwards and let go of Anne Marie's hand. The jungle's din returned. A group of parrots squawked and flew from their perch on the steps above us into the trees. Anne Marie leaned forward and Ramon yanked her back before she could fall. I heard her teeth click and I winced as her head jerked from the pull.

I meant to ask what the hell had just happened but the words would not come to my lips. I knew something had just transpired but what it was, was slipping away. I looked at Ramon and Anne Marie and smiled with an idiot's grin.

"What?" Anne Marie said.

Whatever I had been thinking to tell her was gone. I knew there was something but it eluded me like a dream in morning.

"Hold on better this time, butterfingers," she said.

Ramon helped her past the gap then pulled me up. I had the nagging sensation I had forgotten to tell him something too.

THE SERPENT'S SHADOW

"It's steeper than it looks," Ramon said. "They were made this way. Intentionally hard to climb up and down without falling."

We continued up and stopped near the top, just above the canopy. To our left was the sparkling blue sea. To our right was the jungle, broken only by the road we had driven on, then continuing on as far as I could see, an endless sea of green treetops.

"There," Ramon said. "There is another pyramid like this one. And there, there is one completely covered by the jungle. How many more there are no one knows."

"You could follow the *sac be* and find out," Anne Marie said.

"Yes, yes you could," Ramon said.

We climbed the remaining stairs. The top of the pyramid was flat, about ten meters square and had been cleared of all growth and debris. The temple sat perfectly in its center.

Ramon stepped inside the opening into the black.

"The jungle has touched you two," Ramon said from inside.

I could hear him moving around in there but I couldn't see him.

"You were both born children of the fourth world but you see the world of the Mayan people. You see our struggle. You see what has been taken from us. That is why I have brought you here to this place on this special day."

He spoke like he was elucidating some elemental truth and Anne Marie and I were precocious children who might understand.

"Cancun is an abomination," he said. "An abomination that will spread if it is not stopped. This place. This jungle. Our beaches. Our reefs will all be gone. For what? Ask yourself which world do you really belong to? It doesn't matter the color of your skin. Or what clothes you wear. Which world is stronger? Which world calls to your heart? I think you know, but I will show you. Come inside."

I was fascinated by what he was saying but there was something wrong. What did he mean by stopping Cancun? I understood in a way. I had seen the untouched coast from the water. I couldn't imagine all that being ruined in the name of progress. But something was wrong here. This was supposed to be my adventure, our adventure but Ramon was deathly serious and my instincts recognized danger. I'd always been able to get out of trouble by being smart enough or strong enough or fast enough but this wasn't just running from the cops or fighting back against kids who ganged up on me.

"What do you think?" I whispered to Anne Marie.

"Isn't it great?" she whispered back.

"Yeah," I said, but there was something going on that he wasn't letting on. I didn't know what to do. I knew I should turn back. I knew I should take Anne Marie and run down the pyramid. And if she wouldn't come then I should just go and hit the trail and keep running till I hit the beach.

I was caught in Anne Marie's wake. And we were caught in Ramon's wake. It wasn't too late to just go. I knew inside that opening was trouble and the danger I sensed. I didn't want to get hurt. And Dad always said an ounce of prevention was worth a pound of cure. But this was real. This was my chance to live, to really live. I wanted to run, but I also wanted to know. I wanted a little taste of trouble. I stepped inside the opening, Anne Marie right behind me.

The space was small, no larger than a small dorm room. Some light found its way in from the rectangular entrance we had just passed through and a small window opposite it. The walls were solid stone with a stone slab resting atop them. I had no idea how anyone had gotten that big a block up here.

Ramon stood in front of us, in the center of the room, a stone altar in front of him. My eyes adjusted and I saw it was in the shape of a coiled snake. Bits of glass and stone and shell adorned it and had been embedded in the stone.

In the corner was another altar; it was shaped like a cat, a jaguar maybe. Ramon's saddlebag hung from the cat's head and a few water bottles and a can of paint rested on its flat back. From the way it was turned it seemed haphazardly placed like it had been shoved aside and left there.

Ramon took off his shirt. He held a coconut shell in his hand.

I let out a little laugh and Anne Marie elbowed me.

"Welcome to the temple of the serpent god," Ramon said.

He spoke like he was welcoming us in the lobby of a grand hotel. He reached into the coconut shell and slathered what looked like green paint on his shoulders and chest. He lit a match and dropped it into the shell. Whatever was inside flared and the temple filled with orange firelight.

That did it. Now I was scared and wished I hadn't come. Ramon had made me feel safe. He knew Reginald. He was so calm and under control and so eager to show us a good time. I thought I was in good hands. Now I felt alone in deep water. And stupid. I had to be alert and not make any more stupid decisions or something bad was going to happen. I just had to figure the best way out of this. I looked to Anne Marie. She seemed fine. Was I just being a big chicken?

Anne Marie was fascinated by the walls. They were not bare stone as I had first thought; they were covered with remnants of old paint, dark reds and dull yellows the same as the paint on the jaguar altar. All the glass on the serpent altar reflected the firelight, and the area around it glowed greenish-gray. In the light I realized the workmanship was better than I first thought. Triangles and squares of green and light blue beach glass were embedded in the stone like scales. In the spaces between them were tiny green and white and blue stones and bits of gold and silver that caught the light. I thought they might be hundreds and hundreds of precious stones and parts of earrings and necklaces. The stones on the snake's head were a darker green with red stones forming a line where the jaws met. Jade and garnet maybe.

Ramon placed the flaming coconut shell on the flat top of the snake's head. Its empty eye sockets filled with shadow.

"A serpent god. For the serpent's nest," Ramon said.

He was full on preaching and Anne Marie was eating it up. So I kept my mouth shut and listened.

"We Mayans used to worship the jaguar. In Chi-Chen-Itza our ancestors cut out hearts and placed them on altars like that one as offerings."

I noticed the jaguar altar was cracked and had holes all over it where stones had been gouged out of it. Something that looked like a plucked chicken rested on the jaguar's back. A tuft of red down by the feet made me think it was the fresh carcass of a parrot.

"The chosen sacrifices lived like Kings and Queens for a day before giving their lives."

His tone wasn't all grand and preachy anymore and he was looking directly at us.

"Gods don't want Mayan hearts, right?" he said.

"Right," Anne Marie said, a big smile on her face like she knew exactly what he was talking about. I didn't like that at all.

Ramon darted from the altar to his saddlebag. He took out a loose-leaf binder and placed it on the flat part of the serpent's back. Shadows and reflected light from the altar created patterns on the walls and ceiling that moved with the fire.

"The serpent is mighty. It is strength. It is beauty," Ramon said in that preaching tone again. "It is primitive and a survivor. It is everything Mayan."

The flame in the coconut shell crackled and sputtered. Whatever was burning in there reeked of alcohol. Ramon bowed his head and whispered. I couldn't hear what he was muttering. Something about a sting.

He lifted his head and turned to us.

"This is your time," he said. "Your time together. I want you to enjoy it. Enjoy this special place until I return."

He bowed and backed out of the temple as if he were a swanky butler.

When I was sure he was gone I said, "Come on, let's go."

"What?" Anne Marie said. "You came all this way to just go? Are you scared?"

"Yeah, I mean no. He's just nuts."

"Completely," she said. "But look how cool all of this is."

She put her hand on my bicep and steered me to the jaguar altar. Her hand felt cool and smooth. It felt so good. I couldn't ever remember a girl touching me that way.

I wanted to make sure we were alone so I ducked my head outside but didn't see Ramon.

"Where'd he go?" I said.

"I don't know," Anne Marie said. "Probably down the other side. He'll be back."

"Yeah, back to sacrifice us," I said.

"Stop," she said and playfully smacked me. Her hand lingered on my shoulder.

"Look how cool this all is."

Bottles and cans littered the floor beneath the jaguar altar. A smoke stain that looked fresh marred the ceiling. I couldn't believe that Mayan glyphs were painted on the walls over the ancient stuff. They were different sizes and colors and all over like graffiti but I had no idea if that's what it all was or what any of it said.

"Look at this book," Anne Marie said.

I joined her behind the serpent altar where she was flipping through the pages of Ramon's loose-leaf binder. Inside were laminated pages of brown, weathered paper with Mayan images and glyphs in the same faded colors as what was on the ceiling and walls of the temple.

"Holy shit," I said. "These look like they're from a codex."

"Do you think they're real?" Anne Marie said.

"How could they be?" I said.

Neither of us said anything as Anne Marie turned pages. They looked real as could be. Had Ramon found a codex? Or were we just looking at photographs or some sort of high quality copies or something?

I wished I could read the Mayan picture writing. The space surrounding the figures on the pages were full of the glyphs. I couldn't tell what the figures were depicting. There were a lot of winged serpents and smoke and flying snakes on all the pages. On one page near the end of the binder was a picture of a pyramid beneath what were certainly images of the sun and the moon.

Anne Marie left the binder open on the last page and walked the perimeter of the chamber.

"Look at all this," she said. "I think the paint on these walls is original."

She stepped through the opening and I followed her outside. She walked along the pyramid top marveling at the view of the canopy. I walked right behind her. Watching her. Trying to see what she saw of the jungle. A group of red parrots took flight, their red, yellow, and blue feathers a giant bloom on the warm breeze.

I couldn't help but think of the bird carcass inside the temple. Anne Marie had stopped and I almost bumped into her. She took my hand in hers and then my other and drew me to her with a gentle pull. There we were looking into each other's eyes and smiling. Before I could think or do anything our lips were touching. Our teeth hit each other's and clacked. She looked embarrassed for a second but then we were kissing, again. Our teeth bumped once more but neither of us pulled away.

We kissed on the pyramid top with the sun beating down, the jungle air surrounding us with only the sounds of the birds and rustling trees and our bodies gently moving even closer together.

THE SERPENT'S SHADOW

I don't know how long we were kissing. It felt like forever. At some point we sat down together in the shade next to the temple opening. I was still a bit freaked out by Ramon but no way was I leaving her now. We sat there and held hands and watched the sky above the trees.

After a minute I turned to her and said, "Is today really your birthday?"

She responded with a sarcastic laugh.

"What?" I said.

"I used to hate my birthday," she said. "With it being on Christmas and everything. If you can believe it we aren't very religious back home but every year it still manages to be overshadowed."

"How could it not, with Christmas and gifts and everything?"

"Exactly. And then Reginald goes and plans his engagement. And this trip. That's exactly what I needed, something else to be more important. I'm sorry. This sounds so stupid and shallow."

"No it isn't," I said.

She laughed again. "Who knew this would turn out to be my best birthday? Yeah, I used to hate that it was today but now I think I love it."

"It's a very cool day for a birthday," I said.

"No. I know I love it," she said. "Everything's going to be different for me now. I know it. You ever just know it like that?"

"Yeah," I said. But I wasn't sure.

"It's like when we were climbing up and you took my hand. You felt that, right?"

I had felt something. She was right. Something had happened. I tried to remember exactly what but the details wouldn't come, like a forgotten song name on the tip of my tongue that I knew I knew but could not get for the life of me.

I smiled as I thought about it and felt like an idiot. I let her smile back at me thinking we were connecting. I was a phony. She leaned into me.

"Are you really going home tomorrow?" I asked.

"That's when our flight is. We've been here a week. The happy couple has wedding plans to make, right? I mean really, who the fuck gets engaged on Christmas?"

Her anger was terrible. I don't ever remember feeling the rage I felt in her. Even when kids used to gang up on us for being Jewish and even when Dad once told us what it was like for his parents in the war the pain was always…something distant.

"I'm staying with you until then," I said. "Every minute. Okay?"

"Of course," she said.

"And I'm going to come and see you when I'm in school."

"School. Right," she said.

"No, really. I'm serious," I said. "I'm so coming to see you when we're home."

"Stop. Listen," she said. "Do you hear them? They're in the trees. They're everywhere?"

"What? Snakes?" I said. It was the first thing that popped into my mind. Images of the green snakes wrapped around the tree boughs.

"No. People. Look, there's someone at the bottom."

The Mayans we had seen on the trail earlier were emerging from the jungle into the clearing. They were on the *sac be*, walking two by two in perfect step. Ramon came out of the jungle, in step, behind them. He had paint on his face and his chest and he wore a giant headdress of red, yellow, and bright blue feathers that hung past his back. In all that getup it looked like he was trying to be the priest we had seen on that stela.

He called out something in Mayan. Hundreds of voices rang out from the jungle answering him in unison.

4.

PERSON AFTER PERSON emerged from the jungle. They moved along the *sac be* in single file, stepping in unison until the first person in line, one of the young women I recognized from the trail, reached the foot of the pyramid and stopped. About a dozen people were in front of Ramon. He looked ridiculous with all that green paint slathered on his face and back and chest and in that feather headdress. He shouted something in Mayan and the young woman began to climb. The line followed her up the steps. People kept filing out, one by one, feeding the procession. I had no idea how far it stretched.

"Look at everyone," Anne Marie said.

"Ramon said there were forty or fifty families living around here," I said.

"I think there are more people here than that," she said.

"Come on. Let's just split," I said. "We can go down the other side."

"Why would we want to do that?" Anne Marie said. "They're sharing this with us. We should be honored. If you're gonna bail, just go ahead."

That stung. She was fascinated by their ceremony and my first reaction was to run. I took her hand and squeezed it.

This was my last chance to play it safe. I knew this was danger. Scared as I was I did want to see. To see with her.

"Uh, I was just, you know, looking out for you."

"I don't need looking out for," she said.

We watched the line of people move up the pyramid. After a few minutes the young woman from the trail reached the final step. She climbed onto the pyramid top, walked past us to the temple, and disappeared inside without acknowledging us. Six or seven people followed exactly the same way. The next person, another young woman, followed and stopped right outside the temple. The next stopped an arm's length from her. Ramon was the next up. Green paint from his face was in his stringy hair and headdress. With a smile and a nod he directed us to stand in the line. Anne Marie complied and moved to an arm's length away from the last person. They had left room for me. Ramon nodded, directing me to stand next to her. I didn't move. Anne Marie looked at me with unabashed confusion. I didn't want to see her expression turn to disappointment so I shuffled into line next to her. Satisfied, Ramon strode to the temple opening and disappeared inside.

Ramon called out in Mayan from inside the temple.

Everyone responded by joining hands. The woman just outside the temple held the hand of the person standing just inside. Anne Marie was hand in hand with the Mayan girl next to her. She held her other hand out to me. A Mayan guy was next to me, his arm outstretched and his hand open. His other hand grasped the hand of the girl on the step below him. The chain of people continued down the pyramid, across the *sac be*, and into the jungle.

"Come on. What are you waiting for?" Anne Marie said.

I had a feeling that something was about to happen. That nagging feeling that I had forgotten something was back, spreading uneasiness through my bones. I just knew that if I joined hands with everyone I was going to be a part of whatever *it* was. And I yearned for it. As strange as it was I yearned to be a part. I put my right hand in the hand of the guy on the step. His hand was strong and was no stranger to hard work. He held onto me as if he were gripping an important tool and he kept adjusting his grip as if afraid he might accidentally lose hold. Then I reached for Anne Marie's hand with my left. Her fingers closed around mine and a chill of excitement ran through me.

I stood there in the line not knowing what to do with myself, like during one of those moments of silence at an assembly back in high school or a silent prayer in temple. I was never able to focus on what I was told to or pray. My mind would always wander and run wild like it was doing now. I thought of how the guy's hand sort of felt like Dad's. And how much it meant to Dad bringing us on vacation. I thought of Anne Marie standing outside the club last night. Of her leg against mine when we were sitting outside the ruin at the hotel. I watched the smile on her face slowly growing as she watched me. I thought of how good it felt to be close to her. How good her skin felt. I wanted to feel her chest against mine and her arms wrapped around me.

She blushed and a big smile erupted on her face. I smiled too and a laugh escaped me. She attempted to chastise me with a stern look but the blush never left her face.

I looked to the sky and listened to the breeze rustle the tree tops, to the insects and birds, and the sounds of the people on the stairs shuffling in place. I had been sure something was going to happen when we all linked hands. But nothing had happened.

A little pop resounded from inside the temple, barely audible above the everyday noises. I felt it more than heard it. I thought someone had opened champagne or something vacuum sealed. I listened for it again and heard a faint hiss like air escaping a tire. Then Ramon screamed.

The guy holding my hand squeezed tight. The chain of people tugged and we all lurched toward the rectangular door.

Ramon yelled in excitement. A horrible smile spread on the face of the woman next to Anne Marie.

My arms spasmed. I felt a shock in my right hand. The jolt shot through me and out my left hand. As quickly as it had come, the sensation had gone. I stood there trying to recall the feeling in my body but only an echo remained. I wondered if I had really felt anything other than a charlie-horse from standing with my arms up.

The hiss grew louder then abruptly stopped. Ramon let out a tortured cry, all trace of his excitement gone.

The woman standing just outside the temple stumbled backward and fell, pulling the person inside down with her. The woman next to her tried to keep a hold on her hand but she fell too and their hands came apart. The line shifted. Everyone lost their hand holds.

Ramon stepped outside the temple entrance, his form and flailing arms a green blur only visible for a flash before he stumbled back into the dark. All along the chain, people were letting go of each other and breaking their silence. The sound of their tense conversations joined the din of the jungle.

Ramon stumbled out of the temple again. A big green snake had its jaws clamped over the bottom of his face and his neck. Its long body floated in the air next to him in defiance of gravity. It looked like one of those tree boas but all grown up and thick as my leg. Ramon swatted at it and stumbled in circles.

Feathered wings unfolded from the snake's back with a whoosh. They were red, red as Ramon's headdress. With each undulation of the snake's body the wings grew a little larger; yellow, then blue feathers appeared among the red as they opened. One summer Dad showed me a butterfly crawl out of a cocoon and pump blood into its new wings; this was like that only it was happening much, much faster.

People were screaming. In the corner of my eye I saw Anne Marie crawling into the temple. I knew something horrible was happening but I couldn't look away. The way the snake moved, the way its body cut the air was of profound importance that was eclipsing all other thoughts. Looking at it filled me with calm. Despite the erupting chaos all I wanted to do was watch its green scales catch the sunlight.

The two women who had fallen crawled to their knees and bowed their heads in prayer. Another woman spun with Ramon ignoring his muffled cries as she tried to dance with him. The snake whipped its body and knocked into her. She lost her balance and stumbled backwards over the edge of the pyramid.

Ramon's hands found the snake's head and tried to pry it off his face. A rivulet of blood ran down his neck, a red-gray streak in the sweat and green paint. As he struggled to free himself the snake's wings extended fully. The symmetrical arc of bright red and yellow and blue feathers began to vibrate then became a grayish-purple blur that buzzed and clicked like the flying fish we had seen this morning. The snake rose higher. Ramon's feet lifted off the pyramid top. The whirs and clicks intensified as the snake struggled for altitude. Then it opened its mouth and let Ramon drop. He fell to his knees, clutched his face, and flailed his other arm blindly.

The thing hovered above him with its head facing me. I didn't get the sense it was seeing me or could even see at all. Its eyes were solid black and struck me as something that belonged to a deep sea creature or something that lived in the dark.

Ramon let out a sob and cried, "Why?"

The snake lunged at him and he rolled to avoid it. It snapped at the space where he had been a second ago. Then it snapped at the air wildly. The inside of its mouth was black. Unnaturally black. The black of space, I thought. The black space between the stars. A loud hiss was coming from its open maw. Something about the horrible sound brought my wits back to me and I backed up and lowered myself onto the first step of the pyramid. I wanted to run for cover but found I still could not look away.

The snake flew in small circles above Ramon, gracefully moving through the air like a fish through water. Tendrils of black smoke trailed in its wake. The smoke was wafting from its body and floated sideways, not up like smoke should.

The hiss grew louder. Patches of skin on the snake's back were turning black. It twirled and corkscrewed and rose higher. Black patches on its belly were crackling and bubbling. I thought it was burning but there wasn't any fire, only the black eating away at it and the thick smoke that lingered too long in the air. A long piece of skin starting at its head peeled away and fell off exposing muscle and bone. The two women who had been praying sprung to their feet and tried to catch it. They leapt into the air reaching for the snake, ignoring its lunges in their direction, but only captured handfuls of emptiness.

Skin fell off its head and tail and back but it continued snapping and lunging even though its bones and half its skull were exposed. With a mighty heave it thrust itself skyward but its buzzing wings went still and it stopped rising. Feathers crumbled to dust. Black patches spread over the last bits of green scales. It jerked and rolled as it fell, a withered black shape against the sky; then it was only black dust raining down on the pyramid coating Ramon and the worshippers and me.

I carefully stood and approached the temple to find Anne Marie. Ramon looked up at me as I passed him. His face was marred with gashes. Tears and blood were running down his face. I'd never seen such a deflated, defeated look before in my entire life. The man was weeping. Everything about him screamed confusion and pain.

I felt eyes on me. Anne Marie was standing in the rectangular opening to the temple, watching, cool as could be, Ramon's loose-leaf binder tucked in the crook of her arm. The two Mayan women were looking past Ramon and me to her. Framed in the square doorway she looked magnificent and regal. She was just Anne Marie in her hiking clothes but she surveyed the chaos with such poise. Standing there like that it wasn't hard to imagine her as an image from one of those stelae come to life.

"I don't know what went wrong," Ramon said in between deep, heaving sobs. "I did everything right."

The women looked to him then back to Anne Marie, their eyes open wide and fixed on her.

"Santa Muerte te llama," Anne Marie whispered.

Saint Death calls you.

She had spoken so softly. So quickly. I wondered if she had even said it at all.

The two women grabbed Ramon by the arms and began to drag him. It was such an act of violence I felt a pang in my stomach. Without any compassion, they towed him to the other side of the pyramid and disappeared over the edge.

Anne Marie came to me and brushed black dust off my face.

"Good look for you," she said.

"Seriously?" I asked. "Holy. Shit. What the hell was all that?"

"Come on, let's get out of here," she said.

How could it be that she was so calm?

Behind her in the temple everything was in disarray. Both altars had been knocked over. Green paint stained the walls. Something that looked like a cracked, yellow ostrich egg was on the floor. I couldn't be more ready to go. I turned and glanced at the people climbing off the pyramid and in the clearing.

"Wait," Anne Marie said.

She threw her arms around me and hugged me tight. I felt the cold plastic of the book pressed against my back.

"There," she said.

"What was that for?" I said.

"For staying," she said. "Now I'm not going through this alone."

I sighed and felt some of the stress lessen.

"Ready?" she asked.

I took her hand.

"Follow me down," she said. "Then to the trail and the beach."

We climbed down the pyramid and maneuvered through the people on the clearing to the jungle path. The trail wasn't as crowded but some people were crossing to and from either side of the jungle and others were just standing there with lost looks on their faces. After a few turns and long stretches we were alone and able to run unimpeded.

The horses were in the clearing where they'd been left but were so agitated they didn't want us near them. Anne Marie spoke softly to Ramon's horse and after a minute was able to approach. She stroked his side and calmed him enough to lead him away from the other two. She put Ramon's book in the saddlebag then helped me up. Then she climbed onto the saddle in front of me. We trotted the rest of the way through the jungle, stopping just before the path opened to the beach.

"Hold on now," Anne Marie said.

I tightened my arms around her. She kicked the horse into a gallop and we sped across the beach back the way we had come.

Reginald and Trudy were sunning themselves on the blanket Ramon had set up for them. Their clothes were in a neat pile and they had apparently worn swimsuits beneath them. They were both red as lobsters from the sun.

"Ramon said we'd have some privacy," Reginald said as we approached.

"It's time to go," Anne Marie said.

Trudy covered herself with a towel and scrambled for her clothes.

Reginald squinted from the sun and took a good look at me sitting behind Anne Marie. I could smell the wood burning in that little brain of his.

"Where's Ramon got off too?" he said.

THE SERPENT'S SHADOW

"He's not coming," Anne Marie said. "Let's. Go."

I thought he was going to give us a hard time but he stopped his pouting and helped Trudy onto her horse. He knew something was up. Within a minute we were all riding.

Tomacito was waiting for us at the ranch when we arrived.

"Amigos," he greeted us as we emerged from the jungle trail.

His smile disappeared when his enthusiasm was not returned. We piled into the cab in silence and drove away. Thoughts of everything raced through my mind, Diablo rearing, the vision of all those buildings on the beach, the look on Ramon's face as those two women dragged him away, and that snake...

Trudy broke the quiet to show off her ring to Anne Marie. I listened to Anne Marie humor her but I heard the disdain in her voice. Uneasy silence returned and in a few minutes both girls were asleep.

What had happened out there? The lull of the tires on the road and all the mundane sounds made the memory more surreal. Whatever had happened I had made it.

Reginald lit up his cigar.

"Merry Christmas, gentlemen," he said.

"Feliz Navidad," Tomacito said.

I didn't have it in me to wish him a Merry Christmas.

"I just got engaged," Reginald said. "I'm going to be an honest man."

We congratulated him. He puffed on his cigar.

"You've got congratulations for me but not a Merry Christmas," he said. "You don't do Christmas, do you?"

I hadn't thought he was even paying attention. Sounded like he was talking to hear himself speak.

"No, I don't," I said.

"I don't blame ya," he said. "I told myself we weren't going to have another god-awful Christmas this year. That's when I knew Trudy and I had to go somewhere nice for this."

He thought Christmas was awful? I hadn't expected that from him.

"I wanted to go to City Hall and tie the knot, hell why not? Trudy's the one for me. But she said no. That it's about family, too. And she's right. Know what I mean?"

"I guess," I said.

"Guessed right," he said. "Trudy don't have much by way of family. Been just her Momma for some time now."

"I'm sorry," I said.

"I'm sorry too," he said. "Especially since her Momma doesn't care too much about her, Anne Marie neither. You should know that being the first boy I seen her take a shine to. Oh her Momma pretended pretty good for a while but now that she's old and not so good at pretending anymore it's obvious that she was just doing it for the money."

"Money?" I asked.

"Trudy was a foster child," he said. "The state, or what not, paid money to her Momma till she came of age. That's run dry. Folks that brought Anne Marie, they still send money even though Anne Marie's nineteen. Don't make her Momma pretend to love her anymore though. Merry fucking Christmas."

Trudy mumbled something that sounded like "we there yet," in her sleep.

"Almost, darlin'," Reginald said. "We're going out to a fine dinner tonight. Tommy-cito? Where's a good steak house on the strip?"

Tomacito rattled off the names of some restaurants and Reginald blathered on. I watched Anne Marie sleeping. I thought of all the times growing up I was made to feel different. Mostly around holiday time because I wasn't Catholic like almost everyone else. Getting good grades and being an all-around nerd in hand-me-downs didn't help. But I had Regina and Mom and Dad and later on music and musicians like me. What did Anne Marie have? I stared out the window at the side of the road and watched the jungle give up its hold as we neared Cancun. I hadn't remembered passing so many poverty stricken areas on the ride there. I wished there was something I could do.

We sped past the airport and into the Hotel Zone. Tomacito rolled into their hotel and Reginald and Trudy got out of the cab. Anne Marie stayed leaned up against the window like she was still sleeping but I had a feeling she was awake.

"Come on, Anne Marie," Trudy said.

"I'll be back, later," Anne Marie said. "I'm staying with him until its time."

"Flight's at five in the AM tomorrow," Trudy said.

"You're not my mother," Anne Marie muttered.

"I'm supposed to be watching you," Trudy said. "Come on. Don't be like this."

"You're not even my sister," Anne Marie said.

She had spoken softly but I felt how heavy the words were.

Trudy stood outside the cab, fuming until Reginald gently took her by the arm.

"Come on, honey," he said. "She didn't mean it. Just let her go."

Reginald walked around to the front window and handed me some money.

"Samson. Conan, whatever your name is," he said. "Just see that she gets back, safe. 'Kay?"

"I think your new brother-in-law just made a joke," I said.

Reginald winked and he and Trudy went inside.

Anne Marie perked up as soon as they were gone. I moved into the back seat with her and gave the money to Tomacito.

"She don't need taking care of," I said.

Tomacito seemed much more relaxed as we pulled away.

"How is your family today, Tomacito?" Anne Marie asked him.

"Very good. Thank you for your asking," he said. "It was Christmas. My children are very happy this morning."

"Do you have any pictures?" she asked.

He frowned.

"No camera," he said.

"Me neither," Anne Marie said. "So tell me. What are they like? What do they want to be when they grow up?"

"My son is five. He wants to be an astronaut." He laughed. "Or drive like me. I don't think he will be an astronaut."

"Why not?"

Tomacito glanced at us in the rear view mirror before answering.

"Because," he said. "There is no school where we live."

"Where's that?" she asked.

"Barrio Sante Shepard," he said.

"Does he like it there?" she asked.

Tomacito made no attempt to hide his sadness and unease.

"It is where our family is," he said. "It is all he knows."

"Do you like it?" she said.

"It is off the road before the airport. Cancun is close enough," he said. "I drive. It's good work."

"Is it?" she asked.

"My father worked in the chicle fields," he said. "All day. I thought I would grow up and do that too. Now the plantations are all gone."

"I am glad for Cancun," he said. His words sounded defiant and a little like a confession.

I wanted to say something. Something to lighten things up but we were at my hotel. He turned in. Regina and Mom and Dad were waiting at the taxi stand outside the lobby.

"There he is," Regina said. "I told you not to worry."

"We were just about to go looking for you," Mom said.

"I *told* you he was horseback riding," Regina said.

"Mom. Dad. This is Tomacito. And Anne Marie," I said.

"Hi Tomacito," Mom said. "Regina told me all about you."

Tomacito beamed.

"Do you want some gum?" Mom said.

She rummaged through her purse and pulled out an orange.

"Look. I have this nice orange from breakfast," she said. "You're probably hungry. Here."

She gave Tomacito the orange and a few packs of Care-Free gum.

"Mom, stop embarrassing me," I said.

"He has kids, right?" she said. "Kids love gum."

Anne Marie and I got out of the back of the cab. Tomacito honked *Feliz Navidad* as he pulled away.

"So, you went horseback riding with this young lady and you didn't bring me," Dad said.

"What can I say, Dad. I was a guest myself," I said.

"Anne Marie. Now that I know my son isn't dead, I hope you'll join us for dinner," Mom said.

"Yes, thank you," she said. "I'm famished."

"Me too," I said.

"Dinner, at the pool bar!" Dad said.

"Lead the way," Regina said.

And just like that the world seemed like a normal place again. Or as normal as a vacation to Mexico with my nutty family could be. All the strangeness and intensity from the afternoon seemed another world for a moment. The sun was going down as we walked across the hotel grounds to the little restaurant by the pool. The Christmas lights on the palms were on. The staff were raking fronds and moving lounge chairs back into their morning positions. And Anne Marie, the wonderful girl from last night, the strange girl from this afternoon was sitting down at dinner with us right in the middle of my world. That was the kind of strange I could handle.

"So. Where are you from?" Mom asked.

"Central America," Anne Marie said.

"Oh that sounds so exotic. Where?" Mom said.

"We're in Central America," Regina said.

"I know that," Mom said. "I was asking her *where* she was from."

"That's okay," Anne Marie said. "I'm not used to talking about it. I'm from a place called Tikal. But I was raised in Albany. I go to school there."

"Albany, no way," Regina said. "I go to SUNY."

"Me, too," Anne Marie said.

"You in the dorms or a house?" Regina said.

"The dorms, still. A low rise on Dutch Quad," Anne Marie said. "But my family's over in Troy. The house I grew up in is right by the RPI Field House."

"Rennselaer Poly Tech, I know it well," Regina said.

"Got horses there?" Dad asked.

"No, not there," Anne Marie said. "But my sister's boyfriend—sorry fiancé—lives on a farm up on the way to Saratoga so I'm there all the time."

"Back when David was little we used to go to this cabin up in the Catskills," Dad said. "I tried to get him to ride but he never took to it. You were afraid of the horses, right? What was that one's name…"

"Anything to embarrass me, Dad," I said. "Next you'll be breaking out the Bar-Mitzvah pictures."

"Oh, I think I have some on me," Mom said.

The waiter arrived at the table. Regina ordered sangria and spared me the embarrassment.

A cute raccoon-looking thing poked its head out from behind a palm. It had the black mask and striped tail like a raccoon but its face was long and snouty. One of the kids from the other tables dropped a piece of food and the creature darted over to try and snatch it.

"Oh, look, a coati," Anne Marie said.

She ran over to it. Two little faces, baby coatis, peered out from behind the palm. Soon she had coaxed a whole family of coatis out into the open with little chunks of bread.

"I don't like her," Regina whispered to me.

"What? Why?" I said. "Seems like you guys are getting along just fine."

"She's making eyes with the staff."

"Really?" I said.

"Are you oblivious?" she said. "All the guys. Girls too. Something's going on with her and them."

"You're out of your mind. Where's what's his name—Heinrich?" I asked. "He too high to make it to dinner?"

"Actually yes," she said.

We laughed.

"Alright don't say I didn't tell you so," she said. "I'm meeting Heinrich at the ruin, later. You in?"

"Of course," I said.

"What's so funny?" Anne Marie said.

We laughed again. Dinner was full of laughter. It was the last time I can remember ever truly feeling carefree like that again. There was so much on my mind. So much I wanted to ask Anne Marie. To go over the events of the afternoon. But we just needed to sit. And eat. I needed it. I needed to feel normal for a bit. After Mom and Dad went back to their room Regina, Anne Marie, and I went to meet Heinrich. He was sitting on the flat stone we had used as a bar smoking a joint.

"Thought you'd never come," he said.

Regina sat next to him. Real close.

"We'll let you two be alone," I said.

Anne Marie slung her bag in the corner. We went outside the ruin and sat with our backs to the wall like last night, and watched the sea. Regina and Heinrich laughed and smoked a bit then from the quiet I guessed they had moved on to making out. Anne Marie and I held hands and listened to the sound of the ocean. Sitting with her was nice, I could really get used to it. The best part of the day was sitting with her atop the temple—before everything had gone mad. It had all happened so fast. I wanted to know what she thought of everything that had happened.

"I can't get over all those people this afternoon," I said.

"Yeah," she said.

"One second it was just us and then, wow."

She didn't say anything.

"What're you thinking?" I asked.

"Nothing, really," she said.

"What happened today?" I asked. "What do you think everyone was doing?"

"Doing?"

"You know," I said.

"I thought you understood," she said. "You don't?"

"I do," I said. "I think I do."

She looked at me skeptically.

"They were praying," she said as if I should have known.

"For what?"

"For a miracle," she said.

"So they asked for a miracle and they got a flying snake," I said.

"It wasn't a flying snake," she said.

"It looked like a snake," I said. "Wait. Are you saying it wasn't real?"

"No, are you?" she said.

"No. I know what I saw," I said. "Looked like one of those tree boas Ramon showed us but all big and grown up. And with crazy red wings. But I keep asking myself, could it be a hoax?"

"Nah, it wasn't," she said.

"Yeah, it was too real," I said. "So, come on, what happened? What do you think?"

She was quiet. I could tell she was really thinking it over. She had that look about her that Regina had when she was doing calculations in her head. She alternated between being lost in her thoughts and looking at me. Sizing me up, I thought. Then she spoke.

"Okay," she said. "If you're asking me. I thought we were looking at the end of the world for a second there."

"What?" I said. "Come on."

"Didn't look like the end of the world to you?" she teased.

"I'm serious," I said.

"I'm serious, too."

"Now you sound like Ramon," I said.

"Please, no," she said. "Ramon was incompetent. Unprepared and incompetent."

"Unprepared? That's a weird way of putting it. But yeah, I guess—"

"You were there," she said. "Are we having the same conversation?"

"Of course we are."

"Wait. You really don't get it."

She laughed. But she wasn't playing around. She had figured something out but I didn't know what.

"I'm so stupid. What did the jungle say to you?"

I shrugged.

"I know it called to you," she said. "On the beach when you fell. And when you took my hand on the pyramid for sure. Probably other times, too."

I remembered I had seen buildings when I had fallen on the beach. There were resorts and roads where the jungle and beach had been.

"Good," she said. "Tell me."

"I think…I think I was seeing the future." I said. "In the future, Cancun just gets bigger and bigger."

"And on the pyramid. When you took my hand?"

She was right. I *had* seen something when I took her hand. Now I remembered.

"I saw you," I said. "And Ramon. No. I was seeing through your eyes. I was linked to you. And to everyone else. Who were they?"

"Mayans," she said. "The lost. The left behind. Those from which all has been taken. Those who know hard work."

"Why is it so hard to remember?"

"I don't know," she said. This seemed to concern her. "Maybe people who can't deal with what they've seen simply don't. And they forget or explain it away."

"Was I doing that?"

"You remember now?" she said.

"Yeah," I said.

"Good. Now remember what we were all looking at."

"A snake," I said. "A giant snake in the sky."

That was what I had seen. That was what I had forgotten. On the beach. At the pyramid. Last night at the ruin and in our room. It all came back to me.

"Good," she said. "I knew you were one of us. You knew it too."

"The snake," I said. "What is it?"

"I don't know," she said. "I really don't know what it is. But that doesn't matter. What matters is that I know that it's ours..."

A huge set of waves crashed on the shore. The white bird from last night called from somewhere.

"Ramon said something about a serpent god."

She laughed. "Gods. Really? Do you believe in gods?"

"No, I guess not," I said.

"I only believe in what we can feel and see and touch. Like the jungle. The jungle I believe in."

She was right about the jungle. I had felt it as soon as I arrived in Mexico. I could feel it now. Outside the hotel zone. Breathing. Waiting. Reaching. Given time it would take back Cancun.

"Now tell me why the jungle called to you," she said.

I really wasn't sure it had called to me at all. Was I being a phony if I told her that it had? I thought about it for a second. Being here made me think about who I was. Seeing the jungle and the

Mayan people and the poverty made me feel different. I couldn't really explain it but knew I was going to look back on this trip as a dividing line in my life.

"My father," I said slowly. "He came to the US when he was a boy. Alone. With nothing. His parents were refugees. And first chance they had they sent him ahead."

Anne Marie listened as if what I was saying was the most important thing in the world.

"Only they never came. Dad was raised in foster homes, till he went out on his own. Real young. Most of his family...my family was wiped out before I was born. Where they were from—where I'm really from, I guess—is just gone. You know, World War Two. It doesn't feel like I'm from anywhere. Dad took us upstate most summers. He had a little cabin in this place with people like him. People who'd been through it. That's as close to a homeland as I have."

"Your homeland was taken from you," she said.

I tried to say more but I choked up. I never felt like anything had been taken from me, but growing up, there always was this nameless sense of emptiness. Dad grew up in foster homes. His stories about when he was young were all awful even though they were gilded with humor. The places in our life where our family should have been were empty. No cousins. No photos. No extended family gatherings. I see how Dad filled those spaces by working. By keeping our basement stocked with supplies, too many supplies. And just things. Just in case he'd always say. It wasn't normal. There was a rifle in a case on the top shelf of his closet where boxes of photos should have been. At some point we starting using the supplies without replacing them. One day I remember checking for the rifle and it wasn't there. I never saw it again. Mom started having enough money to buy us clothes from stores. I remember Dad's tears when he told Regina that she would be able to go to college. And the tears when he said we would be going on vacation as a family. I wanted to tell her all this. But the way she put her hand on my arm I knew she knew something akin to it. She'd lived a life like Dad's. She had no one to give her the life Dad gave to me. The life Tomacito dreamed to give to his son.

"The jungle called me because I'm my father's son," was all I was able to say.

"What if you could make it right?" she said.

"You can't."

"What if you could have what was taken? From your family."

"How?" I said. "You can't change the past. You just can't fix things like that."

"But you can make them right," she said. "If you could. Would you?"

"Of course," I said.

"I thought so," she said.

"Is that what the jungle said to you?"

"No," she said.

Tears welled in her eyes. "To me, it said welcome home." A lone drop rolled down her face. "I know who I am now and who I'm supposed to be. I'm supposed to be me. Not who my mom or sister or Reginald says I should be."

She wiped the tear and seemed concerned I had seen it.

"Regina and I, we complain. But we have so much. Mom and Dad gave us the choices they never had. So I guess when I go back to school—"

"Back to school?" she said. "So that's what you want to do? Go back to school?"

"Yeah, but I have another week and a half," I said.

"I'm sure your mom and dad want you to be a doctor or lawyer or—"

"They know that's not me. Regina, maybe. Well, actually that's Regina alright. For me it's like you were saying last night. I think

I'm meant to show people things. Through music, probably. Yeah. Through music."

"That's what the jungle told you?"

"Yeah, I guess," I said. "No yeah, that's what it said."

We sat in silence for a few minutes. I could feel her thinking. I could feel the weight of her thoughts. I didn't dare speak. It didn't seem right. Finally I felt her mood lighten. I don't know how, I just did. I knew she had come to some sort of decision, some sort of peace. But I didn't know what. She shifted closer to me and ran her hand along my arm as if it were the most fascinating thing.

"It tell you anything else?" she asked.

"Like to run off and climb a pyramid?" I said.

"Yeah, like that," she said.

"And get into all sorts of trouble with you?"

"I don't regret a second of it, do you?" she said.

"Makes a pretty good story, now that's it over," I said. "You're the best part."

"Go on. I think I really like this story," she said and kissed me.

We kissed until we could keep our eyes open no more. We fell asleep next to each other sitting up against that wall.

I woke in the middle of the night to more kisses. I was so exhausted but I didn't want to stop. Regina and Heinrich were nowhere to be seen so we moved inside the ruin. I drifted in and out of sleep as close to her as I could be.

I dreamt we were wrapped in xtabentun vines; vines that had crept along the stones and bound us together, their white flowers open to the night. I rolled over. Light was ready to return to the sky. I reached for her. My hand felt sand. She wasn't next to me. I sat up and saw her walking out of the ruin.

"Hey. You're up. Don't go," I said.

"It's time," she said.

"No," I said. "Just stay a few minutes more."

She started to walk away.

"Wait," I said.

"Don't worry. I'm going to see you soon," she said.

"Give me a sec. I'm getting up and walking you to the taxis."

I closed my eyes for one second and when I opened them the sun was up. Time had passed. She was gone.

"Good morning, Pancho," said Lucho the watchman. "Have some breakfast."

He was sitting on the stone we had used as a bar the other night, watching me and feeding a gray iguana. How long had he been there? To see him and not Anne Marie was a terrible surprise. He took a pull from a joint and threw an *xtabentun* flower to the iguana.

Regina emerged through the entrance behind him wearing fresh shorts and a t-shirt.

"Thought I'd find you here," she said.

"Where's Anne Marie?" I said.

"The lady of shadows is gone like the night in the morning sun," the watchman said. "Looks like she left you that."

There was a page from Ramon's notebook being held down by a rock in the corner of the ruin.

"Why didn't you wake him?" Regina said.

"I don't know," he said. "It's not my job."

"Come on loverboy," Regina said. "Mom and Dad have plans, of course. They're waiting."

I stood up and took the codex page. There were lines and triangles in the sand next to it. Anne Marie had drawn a map on the ground, like Ramon's. Only hers had dozens and dozens of triangles and hundreds of lines.

5.

THE SILHOUETTE OF the Mayan ruin broke the black field of star-filled sky beyond the dunes. I tried to recall the sensation of Anne Marie sitting up against me but only succeeded in remembering her hand closing around mine. In my mind's eye I saw us together on a white horse, so white it seemed to glow in the darkness like the white *sac be* we followed through the jungle. We galloped to the pyramid at the ranch, up its steep side, and into the temple at its top. The far wall of the chamber was missing and opened into a great void where the white road continued into darkness. We rode on and on following twists and turns into emptiness. The serpent emerged from the dark, dwarfing us and the road. Its scales radiated color; firework bright pinks and greens were even brighter surrounded by the infinite black. A knife appeared in Anne Marie's hand. She yanked me back by my hair so she could more easily cut my heart out and give it to the serpent. Before she could, I reached into my chest, pulled it out myself, and offered it willingly.

"Somebody's love sick," Regina said. "Love, love, love sick."

"Am not," I said.

"Oh? You're just staring out the window longingly at the place you two had your little moment."

She picked up my postcards to Anne Marie and flipped through them.

"Hey. Put those down," I said and threw a couch pillow at her.

"Love letters," she said and made kissing noises. "Let's see. Blah, blah, blah. Something about a serpent. You really gotta work on your dirty talk."

"Like you should talk," I said. "How's your Heinrich?"

"He's just fine. Thank you very much," she said. "Which you would know if you went out with everyone instead of just moping around the room."

"What's Brad gonna think when you get home?" I said.

"He's not going to think anything."

"Ah," I said.

"Ah yourself. Heinrich's cute. He gets me high. And he's here. Pay attention, you could learn from that. You should come out tonight."

"Nah, I'm just going to stay here."

"Wow, you really are hung up on what's-her-name," Regina said.

"I'm going to go see her when we get home."

Regina smacked her hand onto her forehead.

"Okay, whatever," she said. "I hoped it wouldn't have to come to this."

She threw the couch pillow back at me, knocking the notepad I'd been writing lyrics in out of my hand. Before I could pick it up she dashed over, put me in a headlock, and yelled.

"Ow. Uncle, uncle," I said. "And shut up, you're going to wake Mom and Dad."

"That's the idea. If you don't come out I'm going to wake them up and say you want to have that Scrabble tournament they've been wanting all week."

"Alright. Alright, you win," I said.

"I always do," she said. "Now get yourself together and let's get out of here."

THE SERPENT'S SHADOW

She dragged me off the couch. A few minutes later we were at the taxi stand.

An ambulance sped by the hotel. Its siren was different than back home but it pierced the night just the same.

"What's going on?" Regina asked the teens staffing the taxi stand.

They looked at her blankly. I recognized their faces. Had I seen them in the jungle or just here every day of vacation?

Another ambulance zoomed past.

"Whoa," Regina said. "I wonder what's up."

She ducked inside the hotel. I saw her through the glass doors talking to the guy at the front desk.

"The White Lady. She has come," one of the taxi stand teens whispered to me. "She's here now."

"What?" I said.

The kid didn't answer.

"Did you say something?" I asked and stared at him but his blank expression did not change.

Regina returned.

"Nope, they don't know anything either," she said.

The one who had whispered opened the door of the cab that had just rolled up for us. I searched his face for some sort of recognition or acknowledgement but there was nothing. More ambulances and small official-looking white cars sped past us on our way onto the strip. Our cab dropped us at Estella's, a club with an outdoor bar area where Regina had arranged to meet Heinrich and the gang. Not far down the strip the ambulances were gathered outside the Hard Rock. I didn't know what was going on but it was serious. I saw people wheeling bodies under sheets into the ambulances. The men working on the skyscrapers across the street had stopped welding to watch. The glowing torches they held at their sides threw the occasional spark down the dizzying heights to the ground. The bouncer at Estella's smiled at me as we walked in.

"What?" I said to him.

He kept on smiling and somehow it seemed a hostile act.

"Easy," Regina said to me.

We filed past him and inside but for me the night was over before it began. I questioned every smile and every drunken sideways glance. I couldn't shake the feeling that the staff was watching me, their expressionless faces casting silent judgments. Though we didn't have much—loud music, some space at a bar, alcohol, and food—it seemed to be a feast. A feast we, and everyone in the club, were unworthy of. Had anyone really earned it? It was just a cosmic twist of fate, a coin toss of sorts that separated me from being here with someone like Tomacito, someone who could not. Tomacito's son might never have the opportunity to waste time like this. Tomacito certainly never got to. What about those people with Ramon out in the jungle? They were born without the opportunities our lives afforded that we didn't even think about. I could see why tales like a White Lady who granted miracles were so alluring. No amount of alcohol could relax me. I smiled. I drank. I danced. But I was going through the motions; all I could think of was Anne Marie and I was glad when the gang ran out of steam and the night ended early.

———

THE NEXT DAY hotel management warned all the guests to stay on the premises and not to go off the property, especially at night. They couldn't enforce it but they made sure to let us know they were serious. I knew enough Spanish to comprehend that the headline of the Mexican newspaper in the lobby said that there had been a "gang attack" at a popular tourist club on the strip. Everyone knew it was the Hard Rock. Did they think by not saying the name it was somehow going to avoid the terrible publicity?

THE SERPENT'S SHADOW

Regina and I spent the afternoon on the beach with Mom and Dad. I noticed there were guards with rifles patrolling both sides of the hotel's designated area of beach.

After dinner with Mom and Dad in the hotel restaurant Regina and I went back to the room. I wrote lyrics and beat notations in my notepad. Regina paced and complained that we were doing nothing and that our day's sightseeing plans had been canceled.

"That's it. I'm going to the taxi stand," Regina said.

I followed her. I wasn't going to let her go and get hurt. There were a ton of cabs. Regina waved one over from the queue. I waved it away but it kept coming. The horn honked *Feliz Navidad*. It was Tomacito. Wow, he really was our guardian angel. Always looking out for us.

I asked him about what was going on. He told us that something terrible had happened but wouldn't say anything more. He either didn't know anything or didn't want to talk about the subject. He wouldn't even take us for a ride. I couldn't drag a thing out of him but I just knew that he knew more than he was telling. I shrugged his evasiveness off, figuring he was trying to protect us.

I talked Regina down from her metaphorical ledge and lured her back to our room by baiting her with banter. When I asked about Heinrich she said he had already gone home. Had she even said goodbye to him? Had he meant so little to her? How could she understand that Anne Marie and I had something…special? When I was convinced she wouldn't try anything again I let her mope and finished writing a postcard. I thought I had been writing words but my last sentence trailed off into a wavy line that led to a triangle, like the one Anne Marie had drawn in the sand. Very strange. But I decided to keep it and I put it in the pile to stamp and send anyway. Poor Regina, yeah, missing out on exploring had been a letdown but it didn't seem so bad compared to the reality of New York's cold and snow that Anne Marie was experiencing back in Albany.

We spent the next morning on the beach as a family. For a few moments things felt like they used to be. Just the four of us doing nothing together. Before the sun had reached its noon apex Mom and Dad announced we were having lunch in town because we wouldn't be able to go out for dinner when it was dark. I didn't see how that would make things safer but I certainly wanted to go.

Tomacito was waiting for us in his cab in the hotel circle. He refused to let us travel on the hotel shuttle, a packed minivan that looked very full and very hot. Mom and Dad and Regina sat in the back and I sat in the front of the cab. I noticed the white figurine had been removed from his dashboard. He hadn't bothered to clean the crusty glue stain that remained.

"How are you today, Amigo?" I asked.

Maybe it was Mom and Dad being around that made him quiet. I wasn't sure what it was but could tell something was troubling him. Yeah, with everything business was slow, but I couldn't shake the notion that he had been hovering, not merely looking after us.

He dropped us near the square where the hotel shuttles were parked and said he'd park his cab and be wandering nearby so it wouldn't be hard to find him when we were ready to leave. I offered him money but he refused. Dad made his "I'm impressed" face but Tomacito's refusal worried me.

The vacation time goodwill of most of the people shopping was gone. Christmas vacation. All that forced, fake niceness was bullshit. You could really tell who was an asshole by how they reacted to the small inconveniences of life, even vacation life, like waiting on line to pay for trinkets or to get seated for lunch. Waiting in line was probably the worst thing that would ever happen to most of these people. And they couldn't even handle it without being self-absorbed.

We headed to the rows of shacks along the bay that served as an outdoor mall. The flimsy wood structures were full of Mexican souvenirs and looked like they couldn't withstand a strong wind. Behind the shacks was a low, wide building that housed more permanent shops. The airport's control tower and one of the runways could be seen across the bay. Every few minutes the roar of big planes landing and taking off drowned out the sound of the wind through the palms and lapping waves.

Regina and Mom paired off and headed into a T-shirt store to make a dent in their list of souvenirs to bring home for people. Dad waited outside flipping through a newspaper. It was in English but was a few days old. I was glad Regina was off shopping. I couldn't handle one of our debates right now. Couples fighting, children bickering, and forlorn faces of unhappy families had me forgetting details about the serpent. I was afraid I might be one of those Anne Marie had spoken about... one whose mind couldn't handle seeing something extraordinary. Would I wind up forgetting it all or believing lies of logic that I'd tell myself to explain it away? That would suck. I wasn't one of those people. I looked like them. Yeah, I was from the 'burbs just like them. But I knew I was different. I told myself I didn't have it in me to ignore people like Tomacito for starters. I didn't have it in me to forget something I had seen with my own two eyes no matter how terrible or strange it was.

Stray motions jogged my memory. Stupid stuff. A guy moving his arm to absently shoo a fly reminded me of how the serpent swam through the air. I didn't want to forget that. I didn't understand but I didn't want to forget.

I went into the little snack shop sandwiched between two of the trinket shops to get something to drink. I grabbed a bottle of Coke languishing in the not so cold fridge between the *cervesas* and Squirt brand lemon sodas and brought it to the counter. A statue of the White Lady adorned the register. The dried clay and plastic figure had a white skull face and held a white lace parasol. It was the newest, cleanest item in the shop. Along the dirty white stucco wall was a hand painted image of a serpent. Like a Chinese New Year's Dragon its coils and humps circled the store. The lines were elegantly formed but the colors had faded with age. In the back near the boxes of cereal was its head. I didn't like it. Something about the depiction angered me. I yearned for a more accurate image. I wanted to see the sparkle and iridescence of the scales I had seen. As I gave the young lady my pesos to pay my hand brushed hers. My head filled with a strange miasma. Thousands of thousands of voices. I didn't know how but I was hearing the thoughts of everyone around me in the shopping area; the loudest was from the girl before me. I couldn't understand all of the Spanish but I knew the thoughts were hers. I felt if I just listened harder or tuned in to the connection better I'd be able to comprehend. There was one strange thought, if it could be called a thought, weaving through them all, binding yet eclipsing them. Whoever it was, whatever it was it felt utterly alien. As I focused on it I felt myself flying through the night—no not night, blackness, endless blackness. I sensed sadness, loss and the resolve to fly forever. I tried to tune in better but Anne Marie's face filled my mind's eye. Then my hand moved off of the girl's and all the thoughts and feelings were gone.

"Uh, thank you," I said.

I knew I'd just had an episode like one of those visions I'd been having. But this time I hadn't forgotten. I was confused but glad I had remembered. I used the opener by the register to pry open my soda and tried to replay it in my mind.

"May the White Lady bless you," the young lady said with her thin, tinny voice.

I didn't know how to respond. Was something dangerous transpiring? I didn't think so, but I wasn't sure. I backed outside without saying anything. I had to see Anne Marie again, soon. I didn't think she'd have any answers, maybe she would, but I just knew I'd be all right when I found her.

94

THE SERPENT'S SHADOW

I returned to the palm tree where Dad was standing and together we waited for Mom and Regina. I watched the departing planes on the other side of the bay. A big 747 picked up speed and bumped along the runway before lifting into the air. I pictured the serpent with its wings extended, rising into space. The plane seemed like such a clumsy thing in comparison. I reached for my lyric pad in my shorts pocket to write that down. I pulled out the codex page instead. I vaguely remembered putting it in the plastic bag to protect it, at least I thought I did, but I hadn't remembered bringing it along. I was glad to have it with me. Its glyphs made me feel closer to Anne Marie. I turned it around and around to find the best way to look at the picture writing.

I noticed Tomacito standing across the lane from us outside a booth that sold blankets and rope hammocks. He wasn't watching over us, he was watching me. Why?

"Hey Dad. I'm going to go over to that store to see our cab driver for a minute."

"I'll be right here," he said. "Looks like they're nowhere near finished spending money yet."

I walked over to Tomacito and asked him what he was doing.

"How are you, Amigo? What were you looking at?"

His directness was unusual. I took the page out of my pocket.

"This," I said. "It's nothing."

"It doesn't look like nothing. Come. There is a place I want you to bring it."

"My parents are over there, they're waiting—"

"It is very near. Do you want to know what it is?"

If Tomacito knew something about the page I wanted to go. I waved to Dad, caught his attention, and motioned that I'd be right back. Tomacito and I walked through rows of booths to the low stucco building that housed the more permanent vendors. He stopped in front of a store marked only with an icon of a pyramid and held the door open. The shop was long and narrow and stretched deep into the building but was only as wide as the plain gray metal desk at the far end. Both side walls were lined with bookcases leaving just enough room for a person to walk. A man Dad's age sat behind the desk. He looked like my Meso-American studies professor only a lot more ragged and road worn. His long, thin hair was matted from sweat. Silver framed glasses sat a bit crooked on his nose. His linen dress shirt was stained with rings of old sweat. The wall behind the desk was free from shelves and had a single oversized framed photo of the man and some other people who also looked to me like professors or intellectuals; they were all standing next to an open pit in the jungle. The man looked a lot younger in the photo and his hair was in a ponytail and fuller. In the background of the photo were Mayan workers, who had probably done all the digging, casually leaning against the palms.

"Just a second. Feel free to browse while I finish with this call," the man said absently.

Tomacito stepped back so I could easily see all the books. There were so many. Titles like *Butler's Guide to the Darien* and a *Field Guide to the Birds of Mexico*. I pulled out a book that was simply titled *Flora and Fauna*.

I looked up *xtabentun* near the back. The entry called it an invasive vine and said that it had hallucinogenic properties. Invasive from where? Great, the book had been published in the States. I moved on to a book on Central American gods. I stopped at a page that had a hand drawn picture of *Quetzalcoatl*. It looked like the wall drawing in the snack shop. The next page had a drawing of *Kukulkan*. They both looked nothing like what Anne Marie and I had seen. I found plenty of books on birds and snakes. Plenty about the *fer-de-lance* and boa constrictors that lived in the Yucatan. I flipped through one and stopped on a page about a bird called the quetzal that had long, bright green and red feathers. But no flying serpents. Nothing in nature that even looked close.

THE SERPENT'S SHADOW

I realized that there was no phone in the shop and the man behind the desk was talking to himself. When he realized I was watching he said, "How can I help you today?"

"Show him," Tomacito said.

Did he know this guy? The man was certainly off, but his store—all this knowledge was his. What did he know?

I took out the codex page and placed it on the desk.

"What is it?" I asked.

The man examined the page with a big magnifying glass he produced from his paper-covered desk.

"The detail. The subject matter. The iconography. It's all correct to the period and certainly looks like you have a page out of a Mayan Codex," he said. "Amazing. But look here."

He held the magnifying glass closer.

"There. That's a watermark," he said. "This paper is modern. Very modern. It was made very, very recently. Probably in the US or Mexico City."

"I should have known it was a fake," I said. "I learned in class that all the codexes were destroyed."

"Codices," he said. "Yes, they are all gone. Except for the ones in the museums. You said class. Are you a student?"

"One semester of college down so far."

"Oh, can you recognize the glyphs for the numbers one through ten? And the Rain *Chac*? You know the difference between a *tun*, *katun*, and *baktun*?"

"Yes, of course."

"Not very convincing. Tell me, where did you get this?"

"In the jungle."

"The jungle? You bought it?"

"No. I…found it. Actually, it was my friend's. She left it for me."

The man placed his magnifying glass on the desk and clasped his hands together. He shuffled back and forth in place and whispered in Spanish to himself.

"I think you should leave, now," he said.

"What?"

"Leave Cancun. Go home," he said. "Get married and grow up and get as rich as you can. Forget you ever came here."

"Wait. Why?"

"Do you want to end up like me?"

I wanted to ask him what had happened to him. Something about him seemed familiar but also very wrong. Before I could speak I heard a voice calling me from outside.

"Anne Marie," I answered.

I tucked the codex page inside my pocket and ran out of the shop.

Tomacito followed me into the rows of vendors. I thought I saw Anne Marie at the end, where the shacks met the bay. She was wearing a hat of green fronds, like the one she had on when I first met her. I ran over. No one was there except for an old man who asked me if I wanted to buy a sombrero.

I was sweating. I was sure I had seen her. But where had she gone? There was nowhere to go. Only the rows and rows of shops.

Tomacito was silent the entire walk back to Dad. I noticed the Christmas lights snaking up all the palms waiting for night to wink on. Mom and Regina were walking toward me with a shopping bag full of souvenirs when I reached Dad. Seeing Tomacito and me he said, "Who's ready for some lunch then a Scrabble tournament back in the room?"

Regina groaned.

I spent the rest of the day looking over my shoulder, jumping at every sound and turning at every female voice to check to see if by some miracle it was Anne Marie.

———

THAT NIGHT, AFTER Regina was asleep I decided I was going to call Anne Marie. I read the instructions printed on the room phone and didn't care how much they were going to charge Dad. This was important. He'd understand once I had a chance to explain everything. And if he didn't—well, I was going to have to work it off somehow then.

I'd been to Albany's campus before, visiting Regina. In winter the naked cherry trees and empty fountains and heaps of packed, dirty old snow made the place and all its concrete structures, low rise buildings surrounding one of the four monolithic residence towers, even more oppressive and depressing. I followed the instructions and pressed in the code then her number. After a lot of static the line rang and someone picked up. I asked for Anne Marie.

"Samantha? Some guy is on the phone for Anne Marie," the girl said. "What should I tell him?"

"Tell her it's me, David," I said. "She'll want to talk to me."

"I would sweetie," the girl said. "But she's not here."

"When's she coming back? I'll call back."

"Oh. You don't know," she said.

"Know what?"

"Hold on," she said.

There was static and noise and some muffled voices.

"You really don't know. She didn't come back from her trip," a different girl said. "No one's seen her at all. And who are you again?"

"What? How can that be? I'm her...friend. From vacation," I said. "Wait, what about her family? Do they know this?"

"She's not with them."

"Are you sure?"

"You know her family?" the girl asked.

"Her sister and her brother-in-law," I said. "You know, Reginald the loud guy with the cowboy hat."

The girl laughed. "Yeah. That's them. They came looking here. You said you met Anne Marie on vacation? I bet they want to talk to you."

"Do you have their number?"

"Hold on a sec let me get it for you."

She gave me the number and I couldn't wait to call and figure out what was going on.

"Wait. One more thing," she said. "We just got our last phone bill. If you get in touch with her, let her know she still owes her share."

———

REGINALD ANSWERED THE phone and sounded like he wanted to kill me.

"New York City," he said. "Didn't expect to hear from you. But I should've figured. Where's Anne Marie?"

"That's what I'm asking you," I said.

"She's not with you? Is this a joke?"

"No joke," I said.

"She's not with you? Then where in god's good name is she?"

"I don't know," I said. "That's why I called. Last I saw her was heading to you to go to the airport."

"You're a lying long-haired punk," Reginald said. "Tell me where she is right now—"

He dropped the phone. I heard him yelling and what sounded like pots and pans crashing around. Did they really think she was with me? Some family she had. If my family found out I wasn't on the plane with them they would have turned the plane around.

I heard a woman's voice trying to calm Reginald, then static and knocking as someone picked up the phone.

"Hello. Is this the boy from Mexico? This is Trudy. Anne Marie's sister."

"Yeah Trudy. It's me, David. I called Anne Marie and heard she didn't come back to school. Then I called you. What happened?"

100

"She was in the airport with us," Trudy said. "Me and Reginald and her were on line to board the plane. Then she said she'd forgotten to buy a souvenir for Mom and said she'd be right back. Reginald and I boarded. Our seats weren't together. It was so early. I fell asleep. I had no idea she never came back until we were in the air and I got up to show her my magazine. She didn't go to you? I thought for sure that's what happened. I thought she'd run away with you or something and she'd turn up soon."

"No," I said. "I even wrote her postcards. I didn't have time to get stamps yet."

"This stinks to high heaven," Reginald said in the background. "I'm calling the police."

"The police?" I said. "I'm looking for her. I'm trying to help."

"Reginald can be a horse's ass sometimes," Trudy said. "But I love him. And he loves Anne Marie. He's worried about her. She's run away before. And he's called the police before. Anne Marie is eighteen now. They say there isn't much they can do about an eighteen-year-old girl who has run away."

"I just want to find her."

"I know. I believe you. If you find her let us know," Trudy said.

Was that it? Was that all she was going to say?

"I will," I said. "Is there anything I can do to help?"

I wasn't sure she'd heard me before she hung up. If Anne Marie hadn't gone home then where was she? I had to find out. I was the only one she had.

—

I HATED BEING stuck in the hotel room. The only silver lining was the little Mayan ruin on the dune by the shore outside the glass doors. I feel asleep on the couch staring at it and actually slept a bit. My dreams were restless, full of twins, and two of everything.

I didn't know where I was but there were two of me, also. One me was helping Anne Marie destroy Cancun and the other was trying to save it. I didn't know what we were doing but there were a lot of people with us. There were also two Cancuns. Each in a different world. Or was it a different future? I couldn't tell. One was the bustling tourist-mecca that I knew; the other a bombed out wasteland after some great disaster. Two serpents hovered in the sky. Their black eyes turned opal blue when they flicked their blue tongues. They floated higher and higher, flying in tight circular paths around each other. One wrapped itself around its twin, unhinged its lower jaw, and bit its sibling's head. It pulled itself along the other's body with its teeth and swallowed it.

I woke filled with the desire to see Cancun reduced to rubble. The world doesn't need another city, I thought. The jungle. The coast. The beautiful blue water. These were the things that were true and needed to remain. As much as I rationally agreed with the notion, the thought itself felt alien and not a part of me. I couldn't shake the feeling that it had something to do with the serpent. Anne Marie would know what was going on. I bet she even felt the same. Thinking of her brought a big, goofy smile to my face. I walked to the parking circle to figure out where to start looking. I knew I could find her.

It was really early, so everyone was still sleeping except for some hotel staff readying for the day. But Tomacito was there in his cab, waiting. He took one look at me and instead of smiling back, he grimaced. My light-hearted, jolly friend was gone. This new, serious Tomacito unnerved me. I wondered what had changed.

"Why so serious today, Amigo?" I said.

I thought he wasn't going to answer. He remained quiet for a few heartbeats before opening the door. I sat in the front.

"Saint Death has come," he said slowly, and so softly, I almost hadn't heard him.

"What?"

"The Lady of Shadows. She is the one doing the killings," he said.

"Do you really believe that?"

"I know it."

"You look...scared," I said.

I touched the patch of glue where he had removed the white figurine from his dash.

"I'm scared for you," he said. "You don't look scared and you should be."

"Nothing scares me. I'm from New York. I'm David the Barbarian, remember?"

I wished that would have lightened him up, but it didn't.

"You're going to look for her?" he asked. "What if you find her?"

And it dawned on me. He thought Anne Marie and the one he was calling the White Lady were one and the same.

"No," I said. "You don't really think our Anne Marie is this White Lady?"

"It's true," he said. "I saw her myself."

"Where?" I said. "Tomacito, tell me everything. From the beginning."

He started and stopped a few times.

"She has been gathering people," he said. "People like me. From my village. After the killings she came to us. She promised a new world. Full of wealth and miracles. But I knew she was just looking for...followers."

"What do you mean, followers?"

"She said she would answer the prayers of anyone who would listen," he said.

"Listen to what?" I asked.

"All they had to do was promise to answer her call when it comes."

"That's all?"

"You don't know," he said. "Life is not easy here."

"Why would she be gathering followers?"

"I do not know," he said. "Her only demand is that they go into the road every night and link hands. Only that, in exchange for the promise of miracles. Would you refuse?"

I thought of the procession in the jungle. A few hundred people had linked hands and formed a human chain up the side of the pyramid. How many people did this White Lady have? I knew he thought she was Anne Marie but he was wrong.

"You want to find her? Let me take you. I will drive you. It isn't safe anymore."

He'd done nothing but look out for us. Something was wrong with him but he was my best chance to find out what was going on. I said "Let's go." And we drove off. I didn't like how tight he gripped the steering wheel and wished the grim look on his face would disappear. After a minute, we passed a line of people walking on the shoulder. I thought I saw them link hands, but it was just a mother pulling her kids out of the way of an approaching bus.

We were heading south, away from Cancun. I sat silently for about fifteen minutes before I asked where we were going.

"To my home," Tomacito said.

"I was thinking Alfonso's Ranch might be the best place to start looking."

"Amigo, I want you to see where I live."

He turned off the main road onto a smaller one. After a few minutes of bumping and throwing up dust, we arrived at the place Tomacito called home. The village was a cluster of buildings at the edge of the jungle. The houses weren't much more substantial than the stalls at the shopping center. Tomacito stopped his cab where the dirt road ended. The ground was covered with stones and tires and machine parts. Chickens pecked absently at the hard ground. Two boys rushed from one of the shacks.

"Xavier. Ronaldo," Tomacito said and greeted them each with a kiss on the forehead. "Please tell your Mother my friend I told her about is here."

Tomacito's wife was not as I expected. She was taller than Tomacito and did not look Mayan. She wore traditional Mayan clothes but something about her poise and her features made me think she was from a big city—was Mexico City the closest? Her name was Kristina. She spoke clearly and slowly with not much of an accent. I complemented her on it.

"I hope so," she said. "I teach English in the school in Cancun."

"Your English is better than mine," I said.

"Between my salary and Tomacito's driving we have enough to keep our little farm in the jungle going."

"This place. It is so nice. And it sounds like you like it here."

"Like it?" she said. "You speak as if we have a choice. This is all the opportunity we've ever had."

"Have you ever thought what opportunity there would be if Cancun was gone?"

They exchanged a long worried look. The words had sounded alien on my tongue. I was unsure why I had spoken them.

"You just said that because you've seen it," Kristina said.

"It?"

"I know," she said. "You don't have to pretend."

"You're talking about what I saw in the jungle?"

"Yes," she said. "It is okay. You are safe with us."

"Safe? What is it you think I saw?"

Tomacito stepped between us. Did he think I was capable of hurting her?

"You probably think it was the most beautiful thing you've ever seen," she said. "All the greens and colors, right? Like a humming-bird in the sun, would you say? You can't stop thinking about it, can you? And you've probably developed a hell of a crush on…her. You find yourself inspired one minute and depressed the next. Should I go on?"

How could she know all this?

"What was it?" I said.

"How long was this one here for?" she asked. "A minute, maybe before it burned up?"

"Her?" I asked.

"The White Lady," she said. "This girl you call Anne Marie. We know about her."

"We?"

"Not everyone is in her cult of death."

"Who is she? Tell me what you're talking about."

"What matters is what she's going to try to do next. We are frightened. Frightened like we have never been before."

"Try what?" I said.

"To open doors," she said.

"What? Why are you saying this about Anne Marie? She's not one of them."

"Anne Marie is a royal," she said. "A real royal. That is what is different. She is stronger and smarter than anyone who has ever tried before. She has a chance of doing it right."

"Doing what?"

"Bringing the serpent."

"Do you even hear what you are saying? I don't know where she is. All I want to do is find her. So just…slow down and tell me you're going to help me find her."

"We will. We will help you. I even have a very good idea where she is. Or where she is going to be."

"You do? Tell me. Take me there. Now. Please."

"You have to promise one thing first."

"Anything, please. I just want to find her."

"Then promise you will kill her when you do."

"Kill her? Did you just say kill her?"

"Yes, kill her."

"What?"

"She's trying to bring the serpent to destroy Cancun."

"How could you even think that?"

"I told you she is a royal. She can do it. She only has to want to and try."

"A royal what? She's a girl from upstate New York," I said.

But I knew she wasn't. Anne Marie had told me she was born in Central America near some sort of ancient capitol. One look at her and anyone knew that was true.

"Why are you telling me this? Tomacito, why did you bring me here?"

"You can get close to her," he said. "People will suffer if you don't."

"Anne Marie's suffering now. She's all alone out there. And I'm suffering. I just need to find her."

"You think you know suffering? The serpent blinds you," Kristina said. "You are young. So, so young. There will be other girls in your life."

"You don't know how I feel. You don't know my life or anything I've lived through."

"And what do you know of me?" Kristina said. "Maybe I'd rather that Cancun did not exist at all. Maybe I'd rather see it crumble. But what then? What next? Do you think there are magic words? There is no on or off. This 'Anne Marie' and those she is with, know just enough—just enough fragments and pieces to really…well, you saw it. What do you think a thing like that does? Behaves? Listens to what it is told? In the jungle you kill a beast before it can kill you."

"Anne Marie isn't a beast. And I'm not going to do anything to hurt her. Or anyone. What makes you think I could, even if I wanted to?"

"Because you must," she said.

Could anything this woman was saying be true? I just needed to see Anne Marie. I knew everything would be clear once I did. But where was she? I thought of my last moments with her. Of her drawing of triangles and lines between them.

"Where did you get that?" she said.

I was holding the codex page in my hand. I hadn't realized I'd pulled it from my pocket.

"Did the White Lady see this?"

"You mean Anne Marie? Yeah, a whole book of it," I said. "Pages upon pages."

"This is very bad. Worse than I thought," she said.

"Why? What do you think it is?"

"Instructions," she said. "Detailed instructions. A part of them."

"But it's a fake. Right?"

"It's a copy but not a fake."

"Of what? All the codices were destroyed. Even I know that."

"It's not a copy of a codex. It's from something much more permanent," she said. "We need to find her. Tomacito. Help him. Please. It is even more urgent than I thought."

"Yes my love," Tomacito said.

Kristina seemed terribly disturbed. She brought her hands to her lips and whistled. Four men emerged from the jungle in response. They did not seem like farmers, though they carried rakes and hoes. She said goodbye to Tomacito and walked off with the men. Tomacito took Xavier and Ronaldo back to the group hanging clothes from a line strung between shacks.

"We will go swimming soon, boys," he told them.

We returned to his cab.

"Just take me home, I mean to my hotel," I said.

As we drove I told myself I was going to tell Regina everything. She'd know what to do. When we reached the turn off to Cancun, Tomacito took the road toward the strip instead of the resort zone.

"Why the strip?" I asked.

"We think she's here, somewhere, or is going to be."

"We?"

"My people."

The way he said it made me think he was talking about more than his village.

"What aren't you telling me? How do you know this?"

He responded by pulling into the parking lot for one of the high rise hotels. It was across the road from the Hotel Krystal and its nightclub of the same name, the place Regina and I had almost gone our first night out. The building's modern silhouette was alive with lights and the street was full of motion. A line of people stretched all the way to the end of the strip.

People waiting to get into the nightclub looked on at all the Mayans and workers hand in hand. Then as if responding to a silent cue, the line broke up. Everyone disappeared into the clubs and restaurants and hotels.

"They come out at night," Tomacito said. "And link hands as the White Lady asks. They are practicing. Waiting for her call."

"What about the police?" I said. "What do they say?"

"The police aren't like your police. There is no justice here," Tomacito said. "Not for people like me."

"Don't you want this terrible place gone?"

"Before Cancun there was nothing," he said. "My father slaved in chicle fields every day of his life until he died. Now, there is a choice, it is not much but it is a choice. I don't want to live in the jungle forever. I don't want my kids to grow up the way I did."

Did Dad ever have justice? Did his family? Without him I would have never been here nor met Anne Marie. Anne Marie had asked me if I would make it right for him if I could. I knew my answer now. I would. I knew that making things right was part of life. Maybe it was part of being a dad like Tomacito was. Maybe I would be a dad someday and I would know for sure. I had to find Anne Marie and tell her this.

"Okay," I said. "Let's go. Let's find her."

We drove up and down the strip. After an hour with no sign of her I wondered what we were looking for. I don't know what Tomacito expected to find. What would she be doing on the strip? It just wasn't her. Around midnight we finally returned to my hotel and agreed to try again tomorrow after dark. I walked the hotel grounds feeling even more alone. Regina was sitting outside the sliding doors to our room having a cigarette.

"I covered for you," she said. "I told Mom and Dad that you met a nice girl who went to your school and not to worry. You're lucky I'm so smooth and it seemed like they wanted some alone time anyway."

I went inside and slid the door closed, sealing Mexico and Regina's smoke outside. I couldn't stand it, all of it. The shining moon, the palms, the buildings, the bay, all of it so beautiful and so indifferent to my struggle.

———

WE WERE ALL disappointed with breakfast. Hotel management apologized for being short staffed and gave us free vouchers to try out scuba diving lessons in the big central swimming pool. Unless there was bacon and eggs down there what good was that, I thought. Even worse, I had no way to avoid participating in the family Scrabble tournament Mom and Dad convened. I hated the game but even still, usually I was a champ. But today I was walking into Regina's jokes and taunts like brick walls. The words I kept putting down were incomprehensible, not even English. I couldn't remember why I chose any of the letters. I surrendered and dozed the day away on the beach in fitful bursts of sleep. I was glad when dinner time came around but was not hungry.

THE SERPENT'S SHADOW

"How's that girl you met from school?" Dad asked.

Regina kicked me under the table. I asked to be excused and said, "Uh, fine, Dad."

I wished I had been telling the truth. I wanted to know where Anne Marie was and what she had been doing. Was she even okay? Something inside said she was, but I wouldn't be right until I knew for certain.

Tomacito was waiting for me at the circle. We drove up and down the strip—our new strategy to stop at the different clubs. It fell to me to get out and search while Tomacito waited. I didn't even like night clubs. The music. The smells of alcohol and cologne and smoke. The lights. The uncaring faces. The fun of going out had been being with a group, being part of a gang. Everything else was just miserable.

I searched the crowds for Anne Marie and looked at every waiter, bouncer, and bar boy for some sign they were with this White Lady. I thought we had covered every place we could think of. Then Tomacito drove to the Krystal.

"I remember this place. That first night. The kids at the taxi stand directed us here but you steered us away."

"Be careful," he said. "A lot of her people work here, we know."

I got out of the cab and stood at the end of the line. Waiting with all the decked out people I felt even more out of place and uncomfortable.

"Hey, don't I know you?" a voice called.

A bouncer was walking straight for me. After a second I recognized Lucho, the watchman who had partied with us at the tiny Mayan ruin.

"What are you doing here?" Lucho asked. "Why aren't you dressed up?"

I knew he was a big softie but he didn't look so friendly tonight.

"Hello my friend," I said. "I was told to come here."

"By who?"

"In a vision," I said.

"A vision?"

I didn't know why I had starting talking about my visions to him.

"Uh, yeah," I said. "You smoke up in the pyramids you're bound to have visions."

He laughed.

"Oh yes, you share my favorite pastime," he said. "But much as I'd like to let you in, I can't."

He turned and walked toward the other bouncers at the front of the line.

"What if they're visions of a serpent?" I said.

Lucho stopped. "What did you say?"

"I said visions of a serpent."

"Is that the password for the guest list?" someone asked.

Lucho spoke into his walkie-talkie then unclipped the velvet rope.

"Follow me," he said.

He led me to the front of the line and into the club. Inside, two other bouncers flanked us as Lucho led me to the back and into the kitchen.

"So you are with us," Lucho said. "We weren't sure."

"Well, here I am," I said.

"The White Lady wants us to be sure. You sure?" he asked.

"Yes," I said.

"Good. The White Lady needs you."

"For what?"

"For blood. The serpent wants blood, what else?"

There were knives everywhere. Too many. Chopping knives. Butcher knives. Why were there so many?

"I'm kidding," Lucho said. "There'll only be blood if you don't follow the dress code. I said there's a dress code, right? It's a white party."

"White party?"

THE SERPENT'S SHADOW

"White clothes only," he said. "There is a store in the lobby. Go. You won't need money. The workers are with us."

He was right. The girls at the store did not ask for money. They measured me and giggled as I stood in front of the mirror and tried on a fancy white shirt and slacks. I blinked and found a bloodied face staring back at me. It was Ramon. Welts and teeth marks covered his purple-bruised face.

"She is so special," he croaked.

I turned away and the shop staff giggled like schoolgirls. I thought I recognized one of them from the procession in the jungle. I looked in the mirror again and found only my reflection staring back. I left the shop, uncomfortable in the stiff clothes and with the fact I hadn't paid for them.

Outside the lobby window I saw a long line of people waiting to enter. The bouncers readmitted me through the lobby entrance without question. Despite the line the club wasn't full yet. A few VIPs all decked out in white finery sat in the booths along the side wall, sipping drinks and watching the few people on the dance floor dance under the strobe lights. I was not impressed, though Regina would have loved it. I took a book of matches with the hotel logo on it from an ash tray at the bar, to give to her. If I see her again, I thought. I wondered why I would think such a strange thing. A server carrying a tray of creamy white cocktails in clear martini glasses offered me a drink. I declined.

The song transitioned into another. The new song was very synth-pop: a sparse electric drum beat and a fat synthesized bass line beneath clean rhythmic guitar chords. A sound effect of deep male laughter, that I could have sworn was from *The Dark Side of the Moon,* mixed in with the female laugh from that overplayed Duran Duran song, was looped on top of the music. Fog machines hissed and released white smoke. A pair of white laser beams criss-crossed over the dance floor. The strobes made the people dashing from their seats to dance seem like they were running in slow motion. Bouncers escorted more people inside. An elevator opened directly into the VIP area. Someone tapped me on the shoulder. It was Lucho. He had changed into a white suit and held a serving tray with a single bottle and an envelope.

"Glad you are with us," he said. "And that you dressed the part. Bueno."

"Thanks, you too," I said.

He flattened his lapels and flashed a cheesy grin.

"Drink for you."

"No thank you," I said.

"I wasn't asking. The drink is for you. So is the envelope."

He handed both to me.

I opened the stopper of the thin crystal decanter and took a whiff. *Xtabentun.* The pungent herbal aroma eclipsed the smoke and stale air of the club. The scent of honey and anise brought me back to being on the beach with Anne Marie. Drinking *xtabentun* with her and Ramon as we rode horseback through the pristine jungle seemed like only heartbeats ago. Inside the envelope was a plastic key card and a folded sheet of white paper. On the inside of the paper in female handwriting was the number 2799, the word "come," and a triangle and a few X's and O's like Anne Marie had drawn in the sand the night I had last seen her.

I'd finally found her! Lucho escorted me through the VIP area to the private elevator bank. The doors opened with the plastic key he inserted into a slot underneath the call button. He punched in floor twenty seven then stepped out and stood there smiling his cheesy grin and flattening his hair with his hand as the doors closed. Questions raced through my mind while riding up but everything disappeared when the movement slowed and the light for the 27th floor flashed on with a ding.

The elevator opened into a beautiful white room that spanned the entire floor. Three of the walls were ceiling-to-floor windows;

sheer white drapes covering them let some of the moonlight through. There was furniture, a bed, a dressing station and chairs, but they barely registered with me. Anne Marie stood across the room in front of the mirror at the dressing station, wearing a hotel robe and a towel in her hair.

I watched her watch herself. She was leaner; her face was chiseled and had seen a lot of sun. Something about the way she held herself struck me as... different. She ran her hand along her arm and I thought of a cat smoothing down its fur after a hunt. Her eyes searched the mirror for something then opened wide.

"I can't believe it's you," she said and ran to me.

She threw her arms around my neck. I was mad at myself for even believing for a second that she was capable of killing. She was just Anne Marie, the girl that I knew.

"I missed you," I said.

"I missed you too," she said.

"What happened? Why did you stay?"

She smiled her beaming smile and kissed my face.

"I stayed because the old me was dead. Just a skin to be shed."

"Why didn't you tell me? You know I'm here for you."

"I told you all I knew. As I knew it," she said. "So much was happening. So many feelings. You know. You're having them too, right?"

"Yeah. And I was so worried about you," I said. "I called your dorm. And your family. They're all worried about you."

"You spoke to that sad excuse for a family I left behind in the fourth world?"

"The fourth world? That's home, right?"

"Home is here now," she said.

"Am I of the fourth world?"

"Do you feel like you are?"

"I don't know. Um, no."

"You were," she said. "The fourth world is the world that has gone astray. But you came back here for me. You left yourself behind. You left that world behind. You found me like I knew you would."

"Anne Marie. There are people out there who wanted me to find you. They begged me to get close and kill you."

"Of course," she said. "We know about them but I'm awake now. I'm…me, now. They are desperate to be rid of me. But you, you are desperate to be near me."

"I was. I am. I mean I have so many questions. Why—"

She pressed herself against me and I could feel her body beneath her robe. Why wasn't she concerned?

"Shh. No questions. Not now."

Her lips found mine. We kissed and all my worry disappeared into her touch. She walked backwards drawing me to the bed, our mouths reaching for each other when our steps moved us apart.

She shed her robe and dropped back onto the bed, pulling me with her. We peeled off my clothes, still kissing, still touching, our actions somehow remaining graceful and in sync with each other. She knew where to touch me. I knew where she yearned to feel my hands. Her head instinctively met mine with a kiss when I turned. I was getting lost, lost in the moment; that wonderful lost feeling like a runner's high and being locked in with the band when all else disappeared. One second longer and I'd be gone.

I rolled away from her and stepped off the bed. The sight of her naked before me was one I'd never forget.

"What's the matter, lover?" she asked.

I was afraid. I wanted to tell her the truth. That I'd only been with two girls before and they hardly counted. With the first one I was so drunk I couldn't remember if anything had really happened at all and the other was one of Regina's hard partying friends who seduced me on a drunken dare and I bet didn't remember me afterwards.

THE SERPENT'S SHADOW

I fumbled around for my wallet. But I didn't have protection.

"That doesn't matter," she said. "You don't need it. Not with me."

She pulled me to her before I could say anything. I saw the two serpents from my dream, one swallowing the other as they rose into the sky entwined. All rational thought disappeared and my body knew what to do.

—

I SAT UP on the bed aware that time had escaped me. Anne Marie was across the room in front of the mirror, powdering her body. She whispered to herself, her pale face speaking both sides of a conversation I could barely hear.

"You're getting dressed?" I said. "Why? We're not really going back to that party?"

"We must," she said.

"There'll be other parties. No one will even miss us."

"They will."

"No one will care. This is... our night," I said.

"No," she said. "Tonight is about so much more than you and I."

"Hey," I said. "Come here, please. Tonight was... special to me."

"It was," she said. "You and I, we are unique. I am of the third and you are of the fourth world. Together we can—"

I laughed. She looked surprised that I had interrupted her.

"Sorry," I said. "It sounded like you were going to tell me together we can rule the world side by side."

She didn't laugh as I had expected.

"No one can rule the world," she said. "We can only reset it. And bring it back to the way it should be."

I didn't like the matter-of-fact way she spoke.

"Don't look so afraid," she said. "You're almost there. You followed your heart to me, lover. What does it tell you?"

"That I'm meant to be with you," I said.

"And you are. You and I. The third and fourth world," she repeated. "Do you feel them coming together in us, coming together as they are ending?"

"Ending?" I asked.

"It's almost time," she said. "Soon there will be no more divisions. No more us and them. There is only the old and the new and the old will soon be gone. Future generations will know the new world. They will know what the serpent gave them."

"Not the White Lady?"

"They worship the White Lady but they really should worship the serpent."

"What did we see in the jungle?" I said. "What was it?"

"The serpent, of course. I know you know. I know you hear it calling us."

"Is that what's happening? How do you know? Did they tell you?"

"They?" she said.

"They. Everyone. Everyone around you."

"Do you mean my people? My family. My true family?"

"Is that who they are? What did they tell you?"

"No one *tells* me anything. My eyes are open. I've seen what comes. You're here to usher it in with me. Just like I knew you would."

"Oh god. Ramon's people really did something to you—"

"Ramon? Is that what you think?" She laughed. "I'd almost forgotten him. He meant well. He knew about joining hands. He knew about the sac be, yes. But he didn't know that the only true power is the power of will. Mine. Yours. Every single person's belief has power. Together, that is magic. Shared will. Shared visions. When you have that then anything can happen. You saw...you know..."

"What I saw was a mess. It was...all wrong."

"The old ways *are* a mess," she said. "Here in the old world everyone believed that Mayans are peaceful and weak. And thus it was so. The new world will be a world of peace. But the old world and its delusions must fall first. To make it fall there needs to be blood."

"Blood?"

"Yes, blood is everything. Just listen. You know this."

"The Hard Rock. They say it was you. Please tell me it wasn't you."

"Of course not. It was all of us. My people were with me."

"Oh no," I said. "No, no, no. Please say you're not the White Lady. She can't be you."

"I'm just me. *They* say I'm the White Lady. Does that make me her?"

"I don't know."

But I did know. I didn't want to believe but I had seen the serpent. And now I wanted to forget. I wanted to go back to sleep. But I couldn't. I had found Anne Marie but she wasn't the girl I knew. She was so much more. And I found that something in me yearned to end her. Now was when I knew Tomacito wanted me to strike. But I couldn't focus. Thoughts of kissing her clouded me. Had they really thought that I could kill her? Even if I wanted to? Something was wrong but she wasn't the villain they said she was. She was... awake, like she said. She was different. She knew things. I didn't know quite what but I did believe she had... seen things. I wanted to know and to see and feel along with her. I could just run. I could just leave and go back to my hotel. Go back to Mom and Dad. Go back to being me... but why would I ever do that? Maybe I did have a purpose in all this. Maybe I was meant to stop her. Not like they thought, just stop her from getting deeper into trouble. I didn't know. It was hard to think.

Anne Marie laughed. I laughed with her. I didn't know why. But it felt so good to laugh.

The elevator door opened with a "ding." Four women, all in white, entered the room; I recognized them as the women from the pyramid who had taken Ramon away. They had white powder on their faces like Anne Marie. One of them carried a delicate white dress. Another held a pile of sheathed machetes in her outstretched arms.

"Why are they doing this?"

"I allow them to believe in what is possible," Anne Marie said.

The women placed the dress and machetes on the bed. They helped Anne Marie put on the dress. I found my clothes and put them on. The women each picked up a machete and unsheathed it. Anne Marie picked up the remaining two.

Her cotton dress was simple. Two slender straps held it up and crossed in the back. In the dim light I had trouble seeing where the dress ended and her powdered skin began.

"The machete is the tool of the jungle," she said. "The perfect instrument for clearing away the old. Making a path so the new can come through."

"Clearing what away? What is coming?"

"Come with me. Let me show you."

I followed them into the elevator. I didn't know what else I could do. Something was about to happen. I had a feeling it would be something bad and wondered if I'd have a chance to run or warn someone. But as much as I knew I should, I didn't want to. Anne Marie was so much more than a girl. She was a goddess to these people. She was their White Lady. I understood.

She handed me one of the machetes. The edge looked so sharp. My hand shook.

"I don't want to hurt anyone," I said.

"It will be all right, lover," Anne Marie said. "A snake feels no pain when it sheds its skin. Only the joy of renewal."

The elevator descended. The numbered lights winked on and off as we passed each floor.

"Anne Marie, what are we doing? What's happening?"

Thumping bass from the club bled into the elevator, drowning me out. The music grew even louder as we neared the bottom. The car stopped and the doors opened. The club was full. The dance floor was packed with people moving to music so loud I couldn't hear myself plead with Anne Marie.

Anne Marie stepped into the club and the lights and music cut with her first footfall. Only laughter, the same male and female track that was playing earlier, blared from the sound system. The strobe lights kicked in giving everyone's clumsy movements from the sudden dark an otherworldly feel. Anne Marie and her four handmaidens were walking onto the dance floor, wolves among unsuspecting sheep. I noticed Lucho and the staff, waiters, servers, bus boys, and bouncers standing motionless in positions around the club.

In the strobe light everything seemed to be moving in slow motion. Something was about to happen. Now I knew it was definitely something bad. I screamed a warning but no one could hear. A woman walking past me recoiled when she noticed the machete in my hand. A spotlight flashed on, bathing Anne Marie in a beam of white. The crowd roared and gave her room; they expected to see dancing. They didn't know it wasn't a show. She lifted her machete. Under the strobes it seemed to take forever to reach the height of its arc.

I felt more than heard the crowd's collective scream as Anne Marie's people took out their weapons. Anne Marie brought her weapon down, burying it in the space between the neck and the shoulder of the man nearest her. The blade sunk into flesh. Blood sprayed. Pristine clothing blossomed with red. The club exploded into the motion of hundreds of panicked souls and knives swinging everywhere. A man with a gash across his neck staggered in front of me. I couldn't hear his gags and gurgles due to the laughter blaring over the speakers.

Anne Marie swung her weapon, cutting down the people on the dance floor as if clearing jungle brush. She was wild. Each swing an act of brutality. She stepped over fallen bodies, her saturated white dress trailing blood. Frenzied people pushed their way off the dance floor and were met by Lucho and staff waiting for them with machetes and kitchen knives drawn.

The house lights snapped on. Anne Marie and her people stood motionless, covered in blood, surrounded by piles of bodies. They watched the panicked survivors clamoring for the exits. The laughter track stopped and I heard sirens. In the plain light with the strobe effect gone what I was seeing was even harder to comprehend.

The survivors were mobbed at the front entrance. Lucho opened the back door and Anne Marie's four handmaidens ushered her off the dance floor.

I'd barely moved through it all. I stood near where I'd come in, covered in blood, the machete still in my hand. Anne Marie and the four hurried past me toward the exit. Their hair was slick and wet, a darker shade of red than their saturated dresses. On the ground a woman with her neck slit gasped and convulsed. Anne Marie bent down and slashed her with her machete. A jet of dark red blood spurted and Anne Marie beamed with a savage joy.

"Come, lover, time to go," she said. "We've done what was needed."

"Anne Marie. What? Why?"

She smiled.

She was so beautiful. I understood why they loved her. She had just killed and I knew I should be repulsed but I only felt desire.

One of her women pulled her by the wrist and led her out the door. A policeman had found his way through the crowd at the front. The last of Anne Marie's people were dropping their weapons and blending into the crowd. Someone pushed me. It was Tomacito. Where had he come from? Outside? Or had he been here all along? I didn't like the way he was looking at me. Trying to see into me, trying to determine if I was... really me. He had wanted me to kill her and I hadn't. I was still me, but I wanted to go with Anne Marie. I'd worry about everything else later. He knocked the machete out of my hand, grabbed me by my wrist and ran with me to the front with the fleeing survivors.

TWELVE HOURS HAD passed. Tomacito had taken me to his village. We were walking to a sink hole with his children to swim as if it were just an ordinary day. I slipped off the rock into the cenote's cool water. All the blood was off me but it was going to take more than washing and a night's sleep to erase what I had seen from my mind. Tomacito and his older son Xavier jumped in together. His younger boy, Ronaldo, yelled a Tarzan yell and swung from a rope tied to a tree limb and into the water.

"Put your head under," Tomacito said to me.

Beneath the surface was beautiful. Crystal clear water allowed me to see intricate rock formations that made up the walls of the sinkhole. A huge fish-shape passed under me and I splashed to the surface. A benign face with seal-like eyes and a whiskered nose surfaced a few feet away. Tomacito's kids laughed and splashed water at the massive creature.

"Boys, don't bother the sea cow," Tomacito said.

I watched the giant mammal disappear into the deep.

"A manatee," he said to me. "Today will be a lucky day."

"Where did it come from?" I asked.

"These cenotes are all connected," he said. "There are hundreds of them in the jungle. All connected. Underground tunnels and rivers run through the Yucatan and lead to the sea."

We climbed out of the water and dried off. Xavier and Ronaldo ran ahead on the path back to the village. Tomacito and I walked onto the trail that led in the other direction, deeper into the jungle, the thick canopy protecting us from the heat of the morning sun. We passed chicken coops being tended by people who greeted us warmly. After a few minutes we came upon an area cleared of trees. A low stone wall fenced in about a dozen apiaries. The air was alive with Mayan bees.

Kristina was standing behind the last row of the wooden bee houses. She was dressed for the jungle— jeans, rugged boots, a long-sleeved gray shirt and a wide-brimmed cowboy hat. The four Mayan men I had last seen her with lingered at the jungle's edge behind her, eying me. Tomacito ran to her. I felt if they had been alone they would have embraced.

"Thank you for returning," Kristina said.

Was that what Tomacito told her? I didn't want to be here. I hadn't returned. He had brought me.

"My parents are probably worried sick," I said.

"As they should be," she said. "Cancun is in chaos. The hotel zone is locked down. They will be safe. For now. Long enough for us to do what must be done."

"Do what?"

"Save the city," she said.

"What if I don't think it should be saved?"

I didn't like the grim looks the four men exchanged.

"Before, when I was a boy, things were very, very bad," Tomacito pleaded. "Our way of life has stayed the same and things have only gotten better. The money I make driving goes here. We buy animals and things we need to farm."

"Cancun may not be a place you or I or he would want to live," Kristina said. "But it is ours. And it is all we have. Ours to tend. To raise. To harvest. To renew. The White Lady wants to take it from us. You saw what she thinks of life."

"This place is beautiful," I said. "Where you live. The jungle. All of it. I'm not a killer or a solider. Or whatever it is you think I am."

I understood they wanted Anne Marie dead. She was the killer. No, she was a force of destruction. But she had promised them a new world. Wouldn't a new world be better? I couldn't help but want to know what this new world would be like.

"I think you are someone who can help us," she said. "Tomacito said you were close to her last night. You're not one of them. You didn't kill. You couldn't."

He was right. I could have killed with them. But she was the murderer. She was everything they had been saying. I wished they had been wrong. I wished I was visiting her at school. That we were seeing a band together or a movie or ordering in a pizza while studying. Why couldn't I have that?

"Don't look so lost," Kristina said. "There will be others in your future. I have seen. Don't leave us, all of us, in our hour of need because of what you think you lost."

"I need to rest and clear my head. It's all been a lot—"

"There is no time," she said. "The White Lady is ready. She's given the serpent blood. She will try again. We must act now."

"I don't know if I can," I said.

"But you must."

"Or what?" I said.

"I'm not threatening you," she said. "I'm begging you."

"What do you want me to do?"

"Get close again. And kill her."

"We'll never find her again," I said. "And why do you think I'm a killer?"

I hated the lack of conviction in my voice.

"There is an unexcavated pyramid deep in the jungle," Kristina said. "The sac be leads there and the underground rivers pass beneath it. All the human chains converge on it. We know she will try the ritual there."

"What ritual?"

"She has already spilled the blood. Now she will call the serpent. We will try to disrupt her. In the streets and on the roads. But you have to kill her. You can. She will take you in."

I wanted to turn around. I wanted to go home. Stop believing. Go to sleep. But I couldn't leave now. I told myself I would, but I knew I wouldn't.

Kristina walked through the traffic of bees and stopped at the jungle's edge. Everyone seemed to think this was settled, but I didn't feel settled. If I made it close to Anne Marie again I didn't know what I would do. Tomacito smiled. I opened my mouth to ask Kristina what would happen to me if Anne Marie didn't believe that I was with her, but she had disappeared into the trees.

———

I RETURNED TO the village with Tomacito. Groups of people were passing through from the jungle and nearby villages, heading for the highway.

"Answering the White Lady's call," Tomacito whispered.

We returned to his cab. People were lining up on the side of the road. Standing hand in hand in a chain that stretched in both directions as far as I could see. The sound of their voices was one big murmur, a miasma of thousands of thoughts at once, but I heard something more. The White Lady— no, Anne Marie— had said the serpent was calling. Was I hearing it?

Tomacito knocked me from my daydreaming with a shove and ushered me into the cab. No one reacted to the dust that blew up from the ground when we pulled away. The human chain continued for miles. All I had to do was join hands and I would be a part of it. Tomacito glanced at me nervously as we headed south. After a few miles he turned onto a dirt road into the jungle much like the one we had used to go to Ramon's ranch. When the cab could go no further he stopped, left it there, and we got out and walked.

The jungle bristled with the energy of living, vital things. Countless trees. Plants. Animals. Insects. Reptiles. Birds. If given the chance, how long would it take for it to grow over Cancun, I wondered.

We passed small clearings where the trees had been cut around groups of stelae. Some had been overturned and hacked at. Others had been restored and adorned with fresh paint. I saw plenty of Mayan bees but no people. The dirt road ended. Tomacito walked into the green as if still following a path. He turned and beckoned for me to follow. He moved slowly; he was looking for something. After about a hundred yards or so he stopped at a huge limestone rock the size of a bus protruding from the jungle floor.

He got down on his hands and knees and crawled on the limestone looking for something. After a few minutes he called me over. He had found a hole. It was barely a foot wide and opened into a giant cavern beneath the ground. The air coming out was cool and I heard flowing water.

Tomacito stuck his head into the hole. I knew he couldn't fall in but it didn't seem safe. Then he stood and led me to the undergrowth about a dozen yards away. The scrub and saplings concealed an entrance to the cavern. The rock had been hewn open just wide enough for a person to fit through. A vine rope anchored to a sapling hung into the darkness.

"Are you ready?" Tomacito asked.

I didn't say anything. I thought of my dad. Had anyone ever asked him if he was ready for the things he had gone through?

Tomacito lowered himself into the darkness. I heard him moving around then a flashlight beam cut the black. The cavern was even bigger than I thought. An underground river slowly flowed to where the cavern narrowed into a tunnel. I lowered myself down using the vine rope. As I descended a bat flew past. I lost my grip for a second, slid down the rope then held on and found myself spinning, spinning in the blackness. I closed my eyes and heard a mournful sound. Even my mind's eye saw black. The blackness of space. So much darker than the cavern. The dark of the places between the stars. A black shape moved through the void. A giant, impossible, black on black blur. I couldn't comprehend what it was but I knew it was the source of the mournful sound. I opened my eyes and my feet were touching stone. I was on a big boulder jutting from the water next to Tomacito. Next to us was an old plastic milk crate filled with a few snorkel masks, fins, and flashlights.

Tomacito moved his flashlight beam along the cavern walls illuminating the carvings that covered them. Remnants of orange, and red, and yellow paint, the same hues I had seen in the pyramid, remained on the relief figurines carved into the curved cavern walls. Some of them looked familiar. I had seen them in Ramon's codex.

Tomacito moved the beam to the other side. It illuminated tiny silkworms hanging over the water on gossamer threads. Hundreds of the miniscule insects hung in the darkness, visible only when they and their threads were struck by the light just right. Something moved overhead. The cavern ceiling was crowded with resting bats. Guano-coated bones covered the rocks beneath their roost. Ribcages. Leg bones. Human skulls.

"What is this place?" I asked.

"My ancestors believed cenotes and caverns were the entranceways to the underworld," Tomacito said. "Sacrifices to the gods were thrown into the ones near their pyramids. They are all connected so the water carries them everywhere."

I pictured the network spider-webbing beneath the jungle.

Tomacito held the beam on a carving of a man pulling the heart out of a sacrifice. Snake-like tendrils of smoke surrounded the man's head.

This place had to be what Ramon had used to make his codex. This had to be where he had copied the images from, I thought. The cavern was one giant, permanent codex.

The beam jumped. Tomacito's hand was shaking.

THE SERPENT'S SHADOW

"What?" I asked.

"The White Lady cannot be far," he said.

A bat dropped from the ceiling and circled into the darkness. I thought of the serpent's wings. Bright red, yellow, and blue feathers unfolding from its green-scaled back.

"We could follow the sac be instead," I said. "They connect the pyramids, too, right?"

"But they will be full of her people. The roads and streets and also the sac be. They all connect here."

I sighed with resignation and we put on the fins and masks. The black rubber was cold and damp. I didn't like how flexible and new they were. Someone had placed them here and used this river the way we were about to. Tomacito slid into the water. The current took him, slowly pulling him into the dark. He put his face down and the fins and mask allowed him to float like a frog. He lifted his head and said, "Come on, follow me."

I stood on the rock and watched him float away. Did he want me to float away with him? Was that what I was doing? Floating away?

"What are you waiting for, Amigo?" he said.

If I jumped in I might never come back. I knew I would never be the same unless I turned around right now. I wanted to be with Anne Marie. I had to find her. I knew something was happening. But whether the city was going to fall or whether Cancun prospered and stamped out the jungle was of secondary concern. I pushed off the rock and braced for cold water.

As I moved through the air a vision came over me. I saw green. An entire sky filled with scintillating green scales. There was a serpent so large it blocked out the sun. I hit the water.

It was colder than I expected. I splashed around then managed to calm myself enough to float, like Tomacito, and I allowed the current to take me into the darkness. I couldn't see the carvings but I knew they were surrounding me. I was being gently pulled into

Ramon's codex. We passed over places where it was so dark or so deep I could not see the bottom. I kept my head up as much as I could and I tried to picture Anne Marie's face the day we were riding on the beach before we saw the serpent. The pristine skin of her face as she smiled. The sheen of her sweat in the sun. But all I saw was the rock-hewn face of the woman on the stela in the jungle being covered in white.

—

WE FLOATED IN the dark letting the river carry us through turns that led into other caverns. Hours bled into each other. Some of the ceilings were full of holes where the centuries had eaten through stone so I knew the sun had gone down.

For the first time I noticed the speed of the current increasing. We were approaching a wall but the water continued flowing. Tomacito lifted his head and called to me.

"The river goes under the stone here," he said.

"What do we do?"

"You will have to hold your breath and swim as fast as you can to pass."

"Me? What about you?"

"The White Lady cannot be far."

"You aren't coming?"

"They know me. They will recognize me. You have to go, Amigo."

I didn't respond.

"I know you are not sure," he said. "I see. I see you. But see me. See I want a future. I want a chance for Xavier and Ronaldo. Just like your father wanted for you. I do not have New York City or America. Cancun is what I have. If you do not kill her, she will destroy it."

"I don't know if I can," I said.

"You can," he said. "It's like swimming in the cenote."

He didn't understand. I wasn't sure I could kill her. I pictured myself trying. I pictured myself grabbing a knife but all I saw was an egg. A giant yellow egg darkening to green. Cracks appeared and spread. Shell fell away and a triangular serpent head poked through, its opal blue eyes laced with multi-colored veins blankly regarding the world.

"Deep breaths first," he said. "Then take one big one. Hold it and exhale slowly. Let out bubbles as you swim."

I didn't like the darkness. I didn't like the depth. But I was so close to Anne Marie.

"Amigo, it is okay. Just go down. Swim as fast as you can. As far as you can."

"Go down? That's it? Then what?"

"Then come up. And be careful."

"When will I see you again?"

"See you soon," he said.

He needed me. All he wanted was a future for his sons. He was like Dad. He wanted for them what Dad had given to me. I closed my eyes and a vision showed me myself in the jungle with two men. I was older. My hair was cut like a grown up. I knew the men I was seeing were Tomacito's sons. We raised glasses that I knew were filled with *xtabentun*. I knew I was in a vision but I could smell the strong honey-flavored stuff as if it were real. We raised the glasses. Feliz Navidad, they said. To your father, I replied.

I hated the darkness but I dove under. I kicked and pulled with my arms and swam as hard as I could into the dark. Visions raced through my mind. Destruction. Growth. City. Jungle. I didn't know which were of the future and which were dreams. And I didn't know what I was going to do if I found Anne Marie. I exhaled a small bit like Tomacito had said and kept moving forward, trying to help the current take me where it was leading.

My back knocked against rock. I jerked and started to sink. I pulled with my arms and kicked hard. I knocked into something and yearned for air. I felt light headed and tried releasing bubbles like Tomacito had said but I got all messed up and accidentally breathed in. Water filled my mouth. I kicked wildly. I was sinking. Going down. I reached out to try and hold onto anything that would stop me. I grasped something hard and rough. Unseen things bumped into me. I gasped and gulped air. An awful gurgle filled my head. The sound of water in my mouth. In my throat. In my nose. This was the sound of drowning. Then all was still and silent.

I was floating.

I kept expecting at any second to cough and gurgle and choke but the stillness remained.

After some time I found I could see. The darkness changed to dusky gray. Bones were floating above me, next to me, all around me. Skeletons and parts of skeletons were gently suspended in the water, moving with me in the current, a field of human wreckage.

Was I dead?

Rays of white pierced the gray. Bones bumped together and didn't drift apart. A leg connected to a pelvis. Body parts became skeletons. The skeletons transformed into fleshy bodies just as smoothly as the darkness had become gray half-light. A man with a gaping hole in his chest floated past. Another was missing half his head. I thought I saw the old man who had weaved Anne Marie's funny green frond hat, only his hands were rotted away. Were these the Yucatan's lost? The people Anne Marie wanted to make things right for? Were these her people?

A woman in a gossamer black gown floated past. Red tendrils of blood trailed behind her unraveling and dissipating as we moved. Her mouth was open in a scream. She was from the Krystal. Together we floated through a field of bodies, all of them victims of the massacre. Is this what Anne Marie brought? Death.

THE SERPENT'S SHADOW

Was death what the White Lady stood for? Would killing her avoid more death?

I bumped into an old man wrestling with a six-foot-long black snake. The snake's jaws were clamped to his neck. Man and snake tumbled over and over locked in the same static position as they tumbled. A horrible purple bruise stained the man's neck. This was Alfonso. I had seen his body at the Ranch the day I saw the serpent.

Alfonso and the *fer-de-lance* that killed him tumbled out of my view and the current took me, and the bleeding girl in black floating along with me, into another field of bodies. There were so many. Men and women and children of all ages with faces like Dad's and mine and Mom's. They were dressed like I had seen in Dad's old photos. Many were naked and had spindly thin arms and legs and round protruding bellies. I realized their stomachs were bloated and their limbs were emaciated. Concentration camp victims. Why did they all look so familiar? Could they be my family? My lost family? The family I never knew? The family Dad never had? The family Anne Marie challenged me to make things right for if I could?

"The White Lady lies," a familiar voice said. "Never listen to her."

Ramon floated before me. His face was covered in welts and purple bruises from where the serpent had bit his face, but it was him.

"The White Lady told me the serpent would save the jungle," he said. "And provide for my family. But she lied."

"Anne Marie told you that?"

"She was not the first. There will always be a White Lady. There always is. You have to kill her."

"But you just said there will always be—"

"Yes another will rise. But until then we will be safe. She must be cut down."

"But you were trying to bring the serpent."

"I was wrong. I see it now. I just want my son to live. If the serpent comes everything changes. Everything we know ends."

"What do I do?" I asked. "How do I do it?"

"Go up," he said.

His words made bubbles in the strange gray water. I watched them float up.

"Up," he said. "Follow them up."

The bloody girl in black took him by the hand and together they sank. I watched them disappear into the deep and I found myself taking another big breath. I expected more water to fill me, but instead I expelled air. I followed the bubbles, then my head burst through the waterline at the surface. I spit out water and coughed. I found I was able to stand and I gasped air as my eyes adjusted to the moonlight streaming in from holes in the cavern ceiling. I reached out to steady myself and felt something bump my back.

A body was floating next to me. I jumped and backed away. It was the woman in black. The bloody victim of the massacre. I sloshed away from the corpse. My feet brushed against hard objects on the stone beneath the water. I hoped they weren't bones.

I half crouched, half floated and moved through the bodies as quick as I could to a bend in the river where several tunnels, like the one I was in, converged into a single large cavern. A line of people, hand in hand, the White Lady's people, stretched into the chamber from the tunnel feeding it. Human chains entered the chamber from all of them. All the chains converged into a single chain that disappeared into the dark.

I spit out and tried to quiet a cough. The body next to me lifted its head and placed its finger to its mouth indicating silence. I stifled a scream. The face was familiar. It was one of the men I had seen in the apiary in Tomacito's village with Kristina.

He was tall and lean. It wasn't his muscles that made me think

134

he was a killer, it was his expression. He was in the water with all these bodies and he was all right. No, he was ready. Ready to kill. Everything about him screamed it.

I silently pleaded to him for direction. He nodded at me, then at the human chain.

Did he want to join it?

He stood and moved through the water. I expected the line of people to react. They continued shuffling in place and adjusting their grips on each other's hands without acknowledging us.

Together the man and I climbed out of the water onto the wet stone. I could see the big full moon and the side of a huge pyramid through the holes in the ceiling. The river had led us into the pyramid; it was massive and barely cleared like the one Ramon had taken us to that first day.

The cavern and human chain both ended at an altar. It was a simple thing, made of two stones and a flat slab laid across them. The first person in the line had her hand on Anne Marie, who stood in the center of her four handmaidens, the same four women who were with her yesterday. I couldn't tell if she was in the same dress or if they had spilled more blood.

I wanted to run to her but I saw something above the altar. I couldn't quite tell what I was looking at. I thought it looked like a shadow except there was nothing for it to be projected on; it was just a patch of impossible black floating in the air.

Anne Marie reached into it, her arms disappearing up to her shoulders. She pulled them out and in her hand was a fist-sized egg. It was the most beautiful thing I had ever seen.

Its luminous yellow surface was laced with green lines and veins like a gemstone. It trembled as she placed it carefully on the altar. She reached into the black again and retrieved two more eggs just like it. The black shape constricted. She reached in again and I thought it was going to finally contract and close around her. She pulled her arms out just before the blackness disappeared. She held an egg in each hand.

She centered the five eggs on the altar. They were vibrating. One of them rolled to the edge and Anne Marie moved it back. Its color faded to charcoal gray and it stopped moving.

Anne Marie gently picked up two of the other eggs and gave them to two of her handmaidens. The first woman swiftly wrapped her egg in cloth and put it in a leather satchel slung across her body. Then she strode into one of the tunnels. The second woman placed her egg in what looked like a square cigar box and then into a pack she wore on her back. She followed the other woman into the tunnel.

I had seen this before. In the vision my first night in Cancun. It was all happening as I had seen. Kristina's man pulled a knife from his belt and handed it to me. It felt right in my hand. I could feel the steel hilt against my bone through my skin. It was an extension of me. It knew what I was going to do. A gun would have been better, but I doubt it would have felt as right.

"My lady, something is wrong," one of Anne Marie's maidens said.

"They are too late," Anne Marie replied.

Someone screamed. The cry echoed through the chamber. Sounds of people fighting followed from the tunnels. Tomacito and Kristina's people had come. They were disrupting the human chains. They'd really done it. But Anne Marie was right, they were too late. The ritual was about to be complete. The serpent was near.

The human chain jerked. People fell forward. Hands were losing hold and coming apart. Now was my chance. I could end this now.

People rushed into the chamber attacking with knives and machetes. Ribbons of blood spread in the water. My eyes did not leave Anne Marie. She stood stoic against the chaos taking everything in. If she fell would the new world she envisioned ever come to be? She turned from the altar and calmly regarded the fighting without any visible concern. And then she noticed me.

THE SERPENT'S SHADOW

"Lover you are here," she said. "Look what we have done."

She laughed and shouted something in Mayan. People poured out of the tunnels in response. This was a war. I knew it now but I couldn't tell who was who or what the sides were. Everyone was fighting, pounding at each other with stones and sticks and knives and whatever was at hand. No one hostile could ever reach Anne Marie through the melee. But I was so close.

Kristina's man charged for her. The mob surged as one, like a flock of birds turning at once, and fell on him. Bodies piled on. He had his hands over his face trying to shield himself from punches and kicks. Why had they taken him and not me? I was holding a knife. I was so close to the White Lady.

Another wave of people spilled into the chamber. The human chain was stretched to its limit. People stood arms extended, barely holding on. It was a mad children's game being played out with fists and blood. One side trying to protect the chain, the other trying to break it. Anne Marie's maidens joined the chain, in an attempt to extend the reach and connect to Anne Marie, connect their White Lady to her people. With them joined in, the chain was one body length from completion. Anne Marie stood, one hand on the egg, the other gracefully extended to receive the final hand needed to close the connection. One more body and she would complete the chain and bring the serpent.

I tightened my hand around the hilt of the knife. My head filled with visions. Competing futures, competing paths ahead collided in me. I saw a future without Cancun and simultaneously saw a future where Cancun prospered. My consciousness spiraled into the vision where Cancun had thrived. It had swelled fat on the resources of the jungle it consumed and overran. I saw myself there. An older version of myself. I was with Tomacito's children somewhere manicured and nice. I had grown up and I knew I was successful. Was I a rock star? I looked like one. I raised a glass with Xavier and Ronaldo. In this world I knew they were all I had. I knew Anne Marie did not exist there. I was alone. Kristina had said there would be other girls for me. This me, in this vision, had met them all. I knew I drank them in and experienced all they were, but they were not enough. The rush of a thousand kisses passed through me, but only brought a thirst that left me empty.

Anne Marie calling the serpent brought me back to the chaos. Her mouth was forming words. Mayan words. Then strange sounds that were not words at all. I heard the serpent answer. It was a sound, but more than sound; it was a feeling that vibrated my bones and permeated my skin. Now I understood. I recognized all the thoughts that had previously been alien to me.

Sorrow.

The serpent didn't want to come. It would be alone here. Anne Marie was going to rip it through time and space. It would never obey her. I knew it would try to go home as soon as it arrived. It wasn't a god. Just another victim of the White Lady. Just another pawn. Just a sad, beautiful thing. Like the boas in the jungle soon to be without a home. In my hand I held the difference. I had the power to end the White Lady, to end suffering and decide which way things would go for a city, maybe an entire world.

The chain stretched, every individual body stretching to its limit in the effort to reach the White Lady's hand but they were short. Like Regina and I had contemplated our first night, everything was a battle of wills. These two armies, these factions of opposing dreams and desire, whoever they were, whatever they called themselves, were battling over which of their visions, which of their choices, would come to be.

I held up the knife. The White Lady wanted blood. She wanted a city to fall. I no longer cared. Cancun no longer mattered. I took one last look at all the fighters because I knew I'd be remembering this moment for as long as I lived.

THE SERPENT'S SHADOW

I opened my hand and let the knife drop. I took the hand of the maiden at the end of the chain. The thoughts of the Yucatan's lost, the White Lady's people, filled me. I would never be alone again. I took Anne Marie's hand in mine and bridged the gap. Their thoughts, their collective will flowed through me to her as I closed the connection. My desire, my lust washed away in the current of human will that empowered her.

The egg vibrated on the altar. It held the answers to all my questions. They no longer mattered. The egg was the most beautiful thing that ever could be. Anne Marie was right, they were wrong to worship the White Lady; they should worship the serpent. I knew its secret. It was no god. It didn't care for them. It did not even possess the concept of what it was to care. Still it was coming. Whether it stayed, to obey and bring destruction, or if it retreated into space attempting to span the infinite miles to its home, no longer mattered. I tightened my grip on the hands I held. I was the last link in the chain. I reached into the torrent of will coursing through me. I wanted to drink in and know the feelings of love for the jungle before I was no more. I wanted to touch the thoughts of the lost as they tasted power. There was no wrong or right. Only old and new. Anne Marie was right about this. She smiled and I realized I did not know this White Lady before me. I reached for Anne Marie, I reached for the beautiful lost girl who was once, ever so briefly, my Anne Marie. I was looking right at her but I could no longer see her face. Could she still see me? The Yucatan's collective force of will became a great mindless, uncaring blur that obscured all else. I was disappearing. I could only see white. The white of the fresh paint slathered on the rock-hewn face of the woman carved into the stela in the jungle. The white gossamer fabric coiled around her as she dressed before the massacre. I could feel it around me too. The serpent was real. Though I was almost gone I could already feel it. I could see it growing. Taking to the sky. Covering us. All of us. All of the earth with its shadow.

ACKNOWLEDGMENTS

THANK YOU TO Kevin Lucia, editor of Cemetery Dance eBooks and Trade Paperbacks for acquiring the book to be re-issued in this edition. Thank you for your dedication to the genre, hard work, and patience. I am grateful to be a part of your vision of this line of books.

Thank you to Norman Prentiss who acquired and edited the previous edition of this book for Cemetery Dance eBooks. Thank you for your friendship, advice, generosity, professionalism, years of support, and for making working on the book such a great experience for me.

Thank you to Richard Chizmar and the entire Cemetery Dance team.

I want to thank everyone who has supported me and shown support for the book along the way. Thank you to my family, friends, and my colleagues especially Michelle Garza, Douglas Wynne, Kathe Koja, John Foster, David Wellington, and Sarah Langan.

Thank *you* for purchasing and reading the book.

I am grateful for my visits to the Yucatan and for the people who treated me kindly and showed me their home land.

And thank you most of all to my family, my mother, father, brother, and niece and nephew for everything.

AUTHOR BIOGRAPHY

DANIEL BRAUM IS the author of the short story collections *The Night Marchers and Other Strange Tales* (Cemetery Dance), *The Wish Mechanics: Stories of the Strange and Fantastic* (Independent Legions), *Underworld Dreams* (Lethe Press), and the Dim Shores Press chapbook *Yeti Tiger Dragon*.

Braum's stories are full of rich settings spanning the globe and explore the tension between the psychological and the supernatural. Many of his stories he calls "strange tales" intentionally adopting the term used by Robert Aickman.

His work has appeared several times in Cemetery Dance Magazine and in places ranging from *Lady Churchill's Rosebud Wristlet* edited by Kelly Link to the *The Best Horror of the Year Volume 12* edited by Ellen Datlow.

The Serpent's Shadow is Braum's first novella and appears for the first time in print from Cemetery Dance Publications.

He is the host of the New York Ghost Story Festival and the Night Time Logic reading series. Find him on his You Tube channel DanielBraum, on social media, and at https://bloodandstardust. wordpress.com

CEMETERY DANCE
PUBLICATIONS

We hope you enjoyed your
Cemetery Dance Paperback!
Share pictures of them online, and tag us!

Instagram: @cemeterydancepub
Twitter: @CemeteryEbook
TikTok: @cemeterydancepub
www.facebook.com/CDebookpaperbacks

Use the following tags!

#horrorbook #horror #horrorbooks
#bookstagram #horrorbookstagram
#horrorpaperbacks #horrorreads
#bookstagrammer #horrorcommunity
#cemeterydancepublications

HORROR
DNA
MOVIES
COMIC BOOKS
MUSIC
BOOKS
VIDEO GAMES
IT'S IN
OUR
BLOOD
horrordna.com

www.ingramcontent.com/pod-product-compliance
Lightning Source LLC
Chambersburg PA
CBHW030348180626
46812CB00007B/2799